MISSY TARANTINO

The Feather Forecast

First published by Honeybee Publishing; LLC 2022

Copyright © 2022 by Missy Tarantino

All rights reserved. No part of this publication may be reproduced, stored, or transmitted in any form or by any means, electronic, mechanical, photocopying, recording, scanning, or otherwise without written permission from the publisher. It is illegal to copy this book, post it to a website, or distribute it by any other means without permission.

This novel is entirely a work of fiction. The names, characters, and incidents portrayed in it are the work of the author's imagination. Any resemblance to actual persons, living or dead, events, or localities is entirely coincidental.

Missy Tarantino asserts the moral right to be identified as the author of this work.

Missy Tarantino has no responsibility for the persistence or accuracy of URLs for external or third-party Internet Websites referred to in this publication and does not guarantee that any content on such Websites is, or will remain, accurate or appropriate.

Designations used by companies to distinguish their products are often claimed as trademarks. All brand names and product names used in this book and on its cover are trade names, service marks, trademarks, and registered trademarks of their respective owners. The publishers and the book are not associated with any product or vendor mentioned in this book. None of the companies referenced within the book have endorsed the book.

First edition

*This book was professionally typeset on Reedsy.
Find out more at reedsy.com*

Contents

Foreword	v
Chapter 1	1
Chapter 2	7
Chapter 3	14
Chapter 4	21
Chapter 5	24
Chapter 6	34
Chapter 7	40
Chapter 8	45
Chapter 9	53
Chapter 10	56
Chapter 11	59
Chapter 12	64
Chapter 13	70
Chapter 14	74
Chapter 15	78
Chapter 16	90
Chapter 17	102
Chapter 18	107
Chapter 19	112
Chapter 20	114
Chapter 21	122
Chapter 22	134
Chapter 23	138

Chapter 24	146
Chapter 25	151
Mini Peanut Butter Pies	156
More Pie?	159
About the Author	160
Also by Missy Tarantino	161

Foreword

I began writing the Granny Appleton series for a couple of reasons:

1. because I enjoy quirky characters and animal sidekicks
2. because I am tired of stories that only focus on murder.

I want to read something that lifts my spirits and lets me root for the good guys in a non-death story.

If you feel the same, welcome to the Appleton farm! Here are the books in the series so far:

Duck Down
The Feather Forecast
Robber Ducky
Quacking the Case

And coming soon... Ducks in A Row.

Chapter 1

Of course, I would pick today to wear my brand-new wig. When you get to be my age, with creaking joints and thinning hair, having something that makes you feel younger and more vibrant is a must.

"AAARRRGGG!" I shouted, shaking my fist at the sky as I picked myself up out of the mud. Wags and Brock, my ever-present farm dogs, licked at my face and wagged their tails. A rumble of thunder answered me. Sighing, I wiped off my derriere and rinsed my hands in the nearest puddle, then slogged the rest of the way to the barn.

A chorus of quacks and peeps greeted me as I slid the large red doors open. A big white streak and a smaller dark one ran past me. "Well, good morning to you, too," I said, smiling at the two ducks happily splashing in the rain-soaked barnyard. "At least someone is enjoying this weather."

Peeper, the white domestic duck, lifted her head and looked at me with her shoe-button eyes. The quietest of peeps came out when she opened her bill. She was quite adorable, in a sloppy way. The feathers sticking up on top of her head gave her a perpetual bedhead. If there was such a thing as duck ballet, Peeper would not make the cut. She could trip over air and fall flat on her face. But she was so gentle and had such a motherly nature that you couldn't help but love her.

She turned and nuzzled the smaller mallard by her side. Harvey gave a loud honk and flapped his wings at her. Or tried to, anyway. His left wing, injured when he was struck by a wayward arrow, drooped in the muddy water. He would never fly again. The blue band of feathers around his neck reminded me of a bow tie and suited his prim and proper personality. Except that he was a kleptomaniac. Every high-brow gentleman has to have some quirk, right? Which reminded me that I needed to check his nest for the brass nozzle I used to clean out the water tanks. It had mysteriously disappeared yesterday.

In the best of conditions, farm chores are a pain in the keister. Add in a sea of mud and you've got yourself a disaster. Gus, the donkey, refused to come out of his shelter when I brought him his breakfast. He looked just like Eeyore, only missing the ribbon on his tail. He stood there with his nose down and kept his back to me. The chickens were bedraggled and grumpy. Especially the big Rhode Island Red rooster, Bruce. When I brought the food to their pen, he charged at me, wrapping his legs around one of mine, digging in with his sharp spurs. Before I could get him off me, he began beating me with his wings. "Hey! I'm not in charge of the weather, big guy," I said, gently extricating myself from his grip.

It's safe to say that the only happy creatures at Appleton Farm were the ducks. Yes, it was great weather for ducks.

At least the orchards were getting moisture, I told myself, splashing my way back to the house. I looked down the rows of trees. The newest trees were planted closest to the house, while the older ones were further back. Every year, I planted several new varieties and took out any sick or non-producing trees. I had lost count of the number of types of apples I grew, but it

CHAPTER 1

was somewhere around thirty. The short trees were covered with dark green leaves. I love the smell of apple blossoms in the springtime, but the time between the flowering and fruit appearing is frustrating for me. I am not, by nature, a very patient person.

Opening the back door, I deposited my muddy gear in the laundry room and walked in my sock feet to the kitchen. Even with the dark clouds blotting out the sun, the kitchen was still the brightest room in the house with its soft yellow walls and creamy white cabinets. I switched on the radio over the refrigerator and washed my hands.

"You're listening to WPLY, Paisley Pointe's best radio station."

You mean Paisley Pointe's ONLY radio station, I thought wryly, peeking between the blue-checked curtains. Through the rain-streaked window, I glimpsed my granddaughter, Quinn, in her bright pink rain jacket coming from the barn with the milk pail. I set the strainer and cheesecloth in the sink for her and pulled out ingredients to make pancakes.

Like many of the animals that had come to the farm, Quinn had arrived on my doorstep, broken and miserable, six months ago. Her heart had been broken and she needed a safe place to mend it. Her life in New York City as an aspiring artist had come to a screeching halt when her art-critic boyfriend, Ricardo Barbieri, had written a disparaging article about her work and then dumped her. Between helping me on the farm and her job as Paisley Pointe's groundskeeper, she had more than enough work to keep her busy. I love my granddaughter, but I don't want her to be lonely. Hanging around with an old lady all the time isn't healthy for a young woman. There were plenty of activities for her to join, she just needed a little encouragement to help things along. At least that was how I saw it.

The radio broke into my thoughts. "It's another bonkers kind of day out there, everyone. This is Wally Teller, your weather feller, bringing you the latest update on this storm of Biblical proportions! Get out the wood and start building an ark, folks. This rain won't be letting up any time soon. I wouldn't be surprised if we saw animals marching two by two up Main Street!"

Quinn padded into the kitchen with the milk and began straining it. Her blonde hair was pulled up in a high ponytail, accentuating her cheekbones and milky white skin. She lifted the heavy milk pail easily. She had always been strong and athletic, joining in sports since she was little. Her shirt sleeves were pushed up, revealing the edge of a small tattoo on the inside of her left forearm.

Wally continued, "The warm monsoonal moisture coming off the gulf is mixing with the cool air coming down from the north. The rain will keep coming as long as the strong winds aloft keep pushing this air down. Welp, folks, as more developments happen, I'll be here to inform you. Hey, do you know when it rains money? When there is a *change* in the weather! Ha ha! This is Wally Teller, your weather feller, signing off."

I flipped the pancakes onto two plates and set them on the table along with butter and syrup. I added a jar of peanut butter, too. Quinn moved the milk to the counter to cool and separate, covering the containers with a clean cloth.

After offering up our thanks, we dug in. "At least you don't have to worry about watering the grass at the city park and the golf course," I said, slathering butter over my breakfast. I knew that some of the sprinkler systems were finicky and caused her all sorts of grief.

CHAPTER 1

Quinn sipped some orange juice and nodded. "True, but the rain creates other issues, like waterlogged flower beds and erosion. Also, the dugouts at the baseball field are full of water. The genius who designed them didn't create any sort of drainage. I'm going to have to take a pump out there."

She paused to take her last bite. "Today will be an inside day for me, though, working on some neglected maintenance projects, like sharpening the blades on the big gang mower. When this rain lets up, I'm going to have a big job mowing the grass at the park. It's starting to look like a jungle already. The disc golf club has started complaining about not being able to find their frisbees. Why they insist on playing in this monsoon, I'll never understand. I'm not sure even that big riding mower will be able to handle the job. I also need to tinker with the sprinkler pump at the park again. Ever since it was sabotaged, I can't seem to get the flow rate quite right. What's on your agenda for today?" She took her plate to the sink and rinsed it off.

I reached my hand up and pulled a folded slip of paper from under my stylish new wig. It had been spared most of the mud bath and was only slightly damp. It was dark brown, short on the sides and back, and slightly longer on top with waves instead of curls. At 67 years old, I was having problems with thinning hair and wigs had seemed the logical solution. I had quite a large collection of them and loved being able to change my look with my moods. It wasn't a bad place to keep small objects, when short on pockets.

"Well, let's see. I've got several egg deliveries to make today. I need to stop at the feed store as well. We're low on chicken feed. I think I'll grab a bag of oyster shells. I've noticed that the eggshells are getting a little thin. Time to add a supplement to their feed. Did you need me to pick up anything?" When Quinn shook her head, I folded the list and put it back, patting my hair into place.

Quinn gave me a quick hug. "See you at lunchtime." Donning her rain gear, she headed back out into the downpour.

Checking the time, I decided to do some baking. The feed store didn't open until nine, anyway.

Chapter 2

The foul weather hadn't had a negative effect on my flock of laying hens. In fact, they had upped their production. I guess when you can't go outside and chase grasshoppers, the only thing left to do is lay eggs. Luckily, I had several regular customers in town. I packed a large crate with eggs and hauled them out the back door to my golf cart.

Before Quinn had arrived on the farm, my golf cart had been a plain old white boring thing. For my birthday, she'd given it a custom paint job. Now it looked like the Fourth of July on wheels. Large waving red and white stripes ran down the sides and the roof sported a blue field covered with white stars. It was a zippy little thing, too. It allowed me to take shortcuts across the grass in the city park, which earned me a lot of dirty looks.

The second I opened my squeaky screen door, another item on the long list of repairs the farm needed, Harvey and Peeper came running. (The one thing those two ducks love more than playing in puddles is going for rides to town. I think they are even more social than I am, and I love talking to everyone!) Quacking, peeping, and flapping, they couldn't wait for me to lift the plastic flap so they could get up on the front seat. They sat there, looking expectantly at me.

"Hold your horses, you two," I said. "I've got to go back in the house for a second load. Be patient, please." They just stared at me with their dark liquid eyes. I swear they were smiling at me.

Soon we were splashing out of the farm yard and down the long lane that led to the main road. We passed between the rows of fruit trees that my late husband, Chet, had planted. Not a tree trunk was even the slightest bit out of line with the others. Each row was labeled with a metal sign that was marked with a number, which corresponded with the variety of apples that were growing there. I inspected the trees closest to the road as we drove slowly up the dirt track. If this rain didn't let up soon, there would be root rot to contend with.

Turning right onto a larger dirt road, I headed toward town. The tires slipped and spun in the thick slimy mud. I had to drive slowly and try to keep to the center of the road, otherwise, I was afraid we would end up sliding into the overflowing irrigation ditch that paralleled the road.

The parking lot in front of Paisley Farm and Feed was unusually full for a Monday morning. I drove around a bit before finding a spot. I squeezed my tiny cart in between two trucks right in front of the building, not sure who they belonged to. They were both a muddy mess.

I clomped my way across the old-fashioned wooden porch in front of the store. It reminded me of how cowboy boots sounded on boardwalks in western movies. All that was missing was the jingling noise from a pair of spurs. Of course, the movies didn't have flapping webbed feet or quacking. A little bell jangled when I pushed open the glass door. I was a little disappointed that it wasn't one of those swinging saloon doors and that I wasn't wearing a Stetson I could thumb back on my head as I glanced around the interior.

Modern fluorescent lighting further ruined my mental image,

along with metal shelving and industrial linoleum flooring.

Peeper announced our arrival with a soft peep and three shakes of her big white wings. Harvey ducked around her, quacking and snaking his head under the shelves, looking for loot. Heads turned to take in our unusual parade as we made our way past the gardening tools and welding equipment. I approached the feed counter at the back of the store and looked around in surprise. It seemed like everyone I knew was getting orders filled. I nodded to Chris Dodson, the big dairyman from the other side of Paisley Pointe, sitting on one of the stools in front of the counter. On the seat right next to him was Sid Foley, who owned the farm across the road from me. I hire his boys to help me harvest apples in the fall. Nice quiet family. His wife, Celeste, sings in our church choir.

On the opposite end of the counter, dominating the poor clerk's attention was Wendel Watson. He had opted to lean his big sloppy self on the counter rather than sit, and it looked like he was prepared to stay there all day. I hoped that I wouldn't have to look at the gap between the bottom of his soiled t-shirt and his sagging pants for too long.

Mentally rolling my eyes, I shifted from one foot to the other. What I had hoped would be a quick stop was obviously going to turn into a test of my patience. In my experience, farmers are professional talkers. My theory is that it is due to those long hours spent cooped up alone in the cab of a tractor. They save up their words and spend them on their trips to town. Kind of like a kid saving up their allowance to buy pop and candy.

Looking around for something to occupy myself, I spotted a brightly decorated box right in the center of the counter. It was covered with yellow paper and had gold metallic streamers trailing off the bottom. In bright red letters were the words:

"The sun'll come out tomorrow."

Pointing to the box, I asked Chris, "What's this about?"

He looked at me like I had just crawled out from under a rock. "Don't you listen to WPLY? There's a big contest going on. Just started today."

"I do listen, but with the rain, chores took longer than usual. Must've missed the announcement."

Sid chimed in. "Everyone's so blasted sick of this rain, someone decided to give people a chance to win a weekend getaway to Florida."

"All the businesses in town are in on it. A different store every day has the box," Chris said, pointing a cracked and calloused finger at the container. "Tonight, they'll announce the winner."

"The winner of the trip? After only one day?" I asked. I glanced around to check on my two feathered companions. They were camped out under Sid's stool.

Sid shook his head. "No. Not the whole contest, the winner of today's prize. Everyone who enters each day gets their name put in the big drawing this weekend."

I squinted at the box. "What's today's prize?"

"A five-pound bag of sunflower seeds," came a deep voice from behind me. I turned to see Tyler Flanders, the owner of Paisley Farm and Feed, coming up the aisle. He had a 50-pound bag of dog food propped on one shoulder like it was nothing. He was a slender man, average height, with a Fu Manchu mustache, which was very fitting, as he was the chief of Paisley Pointe's volunteer fire department.

"Are you going to put your name in for it, Granny?" Tyler asked. "Wouldn't you like to get out from under these gloomy clouds and lay in the sun for a few days? About the only good thing about this weather is that the fire danger is practically non-existent."

I moved to the counter, picked up a card, and wrote my name on it. Of course, I wanted to win. Who wouldn't? Dropping my entry into the box, I asked, "What other stores are part of this brilliant plan?" I could feel my spirits lifting just a little.

"That's the kicker. You have to listen to the radio each morning to find out what store is having a giveaway," said Tyler. He plopped the dog food down on the floor next to the counter. "So many business owners signed up for this, there are two chances to win every day."

Wendel, the counter leaner, finally finished his transaction and ambled off to get his truck around back to the loading dock. The clerk moved over to talk to the dairyman.

Harvey and Peeper were still snuggled under Sid's stool. Little sounds of contentment came from each of them, as if they approved of the contest, too. I noticed something sticking out from under Harvey's good wing. It was bright silver. Bending down, I pulled out a long screw. I sighed as I set it on the counter.

Sid laughed. "I've never seen anything like that. Those ducks are amazing. How'd you train them?"

"I didn't. They just love to come with me when I have errands to run. Harvey here has a tendency to hoard shiny objects. I have to keep a close eye on him. We don't want to be accused of theft, now, do we?" I gave him a stern look.

Tyer walked behind the counter. "The other place to enter today is Dusty's Auto Care. I believe he's giving away a sunshade for your car. Not sure how much good it'd do you in your snazzy little golf cart." All the men chuckled.

As Tyler and I were hauling my supplies outside, an old Toyota RAV4 pulled up in the space next to me. Like every other vehicle in the parking lot, it was covered with mud. But this one was by far the worst. It had mud caked in the wheels, over the hood, and on the roof. The windshield was streaked where the driver had obviously made an unsuccessful attempt at cleaning it. I wasn't confident that they could see much through it. The door opened and a short man wearing a bulky blue windbreaker hopped out. The jacket was at least two sizes too big for Wally Teller. His bare head was receding prematurely. His hazel eyes sparkled and he grinned from ear to ear.

"Tyler Flanders, just the man I was hoping to run into on this dreary day." Turning to me he said, "Great weather for ducks, though. Right, Granny?" He slammed the door shut and headed toward us.

"Hello, Wally," I said. "It may be good for the ducks, but not so much for the rest of us. Lately, your forecasts have been lacking in specifics. Do you have any idea when we can expect the sun to make an appearance?"

Wally studied his fingernails, which I noticed were none too clean. "Welp, the weather models don't seem to agree on when that will be, so I can't predict that with any sort of confidence. But they do concur on the fact that it won't be any time soon."

We moved back onto the porch under the awning as thunder rumbled overhead. "At least the wind isn't blowing the rain sideways," I said. I watched Peeper and Harvey checking out the puddles next to Wally's rig.

Tyler laughed and stroked his mustache. "Way to look on the bright side, Granny. I'm so sick of this weather, but you're right, it could be worse." Turning to Wally, he said, "What'd you need to see me about?"

"Dog umbrellas!" Wally said proudly. He unzipped his windbreaker and pulled out a child-sized umbrella sporting yellow ducks on a white background. It was attached to a large brown stuffed animal. "You fit the harness around your dog's middle and voila! Your pet can go do its business without getting wet." It didn't seem possible, but I think his grin had gotten even bigger. He demonstrated by opening the umbrella and setting the toy on the wooden porch.

Taking a step back, Wally put his hands on his hips. "Well, what do you think? Do you love it?" His grin disappeared and he got serious. "I can make several different sizes and colors. I was hoping you'd let me set up a display and sell them here in the feed store. The ladies, expecially, are going to love these, right, Granny?" He turned his 100-watt smile in my direction.

I pressed my lips together to both keep from smiling and from correcting his grammar. I was trying to imagine my two mutts, Wags and Brock, wearing one of Wally's contraptions as they made their rounds of the farm. Those umbrellas wouldn't last two minutes before my dogs broke them or had torn them off. Maybe someone's prissy little designer dog would wear it to go tinkle in the rain, but not working dogs like mine.

Tyler coughed and said, "Well, Wally, these are certainly ... unique. I can't say as my customers are the right ... um ... demographic ... for your product. I'm afraid I'm going to have to pass on this one." He picked up the last bags of chicken feed and stepped around the dog and umbrella.

Wally's face fell and he sighed. I patted his arm and said, "They're really cute, though, Wally." Calling the ducks, I pulled the hood of my raincoat over my head and stepped off the porch.

Chapter 3

As I drove around town making my egg deliveries, I attempted to miss the worst of the puddles. My golf cart was equipped with clear plastic sides that rolled down and snapped into place, but they weren't a perfect solution. Some water still made it inside. I'm sure I looked like a student driver, weaving all over the road. I just hoped that I wouldn't get pulled over by one of Paisley Pointe's police officers.

Because I was paying such close attention to the road, I failed to see the old rusty camper van. It blew through the stop sign to my right and cut in front of me. I caught a flash of white out of the corner of my eye and swerved to the left just in time. That was the upside. The downside was that I hit a particularly large pothole and my poor golf cart lost control. I fought the wheel and managed to keep it from spinning out. The ducks fell off the seat and landed in very unbecoming poses on the floorboards, quacking up a storm.

"It's not my fault," I told them. I gestured out the window at the disappearing tail lights. "That idiot didn't stop." Fearing damage, I immediately headed to my mechanic.

Driving slowly, I made it to Dusty's Garage without further incident. The small, two-bay cinder block building didn't have any sort of protective awning in front, so I parked as close as

I could get. The lot surrounding the building was filled with vehicles either waiting for service or ready to be picked up. I managed to snag a spot almost in front of the office attached to the right side of the garage bays.

Dusty himself was sitting behind the short counter when I let myself in. Somewhere in the back a door chime sounded. I held the door for the ducks, who quacked and peeped excitedly. "Well, howdy, Granny and friends!" Dusty said, reaching across the counter to shake my hand, which disappeared inside his giant paw. He could have given James Earl Jones a run for his money as the voice of Darth Vader. Gentle giant described Dusty to a T. His dark blue work shirt strained against his broad chest and shoulders.

"Are you here to win the snazzy sun visor, or does your hot rod need a tune-up?" he asked. He wiggled his eyebrows at me. His dark complexion was sprinkled with freckles that made him look younger than his 60 years. From out in the garage area came the sound of air tools.

"Originally, I was only coming for the contest," I admitted, "but I just had an encounter with a pothole. Do you have time to look at my wheel?"

Dusty picked up a card and turned to search for a pen among the paperwork and Little League trophies scattered on his desk. He came around the counter and handed them to me. "Of course, I've got time for you. I can't think of anything I'd rather do than to help a damsel in distress." He bowed from the waist and pretended to sweep a hat off his curly gray head. "You and your entourage just make yourselves comfy and I'll be back in two shakes of a lamb's tail."

He left out the front door while I headed over to the low black vinyl couch next to the water cooler. The ducks wandered around, poking their bills into every nook and cranny. I kept a careful eye on Harvey. The last time we were in here, he tried to make off with a tire pressure gauge. Old '80s rock music was coming from the speakers set high in the wall. Next to the sound system was a poster advertising some kind of regional drone flying competition.

The door next to the couch opened and a young man wearing the same blue work shirt as Dusty came in. His blonde hair stuck out from under the greasy ball cap that he wore backward. He was wiping his hands on a red rag and whistling. The name embroidered over his pocket said 'Jack'. I watched as he walked around the coffee table to the water cooler and filled a cup, drinking the whole thing in one gulp. He filled it again and turned around.

"Hey," he said, jumping enough to spill some water on his shirt. "Sorry. Didn't see you there."

"Hi," I said, sizing him up. He looked to be about Quinn's age. He was obviously good at working with his hands. He was attractive, but not afraid to get dirty. I took an instant liking to him. Maybe Quinn would, too. "I'm Irma Appleton. Nice to meet you."

Smiling sheepishly, the young man said, "I'm Jack. It's my first week on the job. Trying to impress the boss, you know. Guess I was just too focused to remember my manners. Nice to meet you, Ms. Appleton." He wiped his hand again and held it out.

Ooh, polite, too. Give the boy another point. "Everyone around here calls me Granny. Did you just move here, Jack?"

"I'm from up the road in Kirby, actually. I just graduated from tech school. Hey, you must own that sweet golf cart Dusty just brought in."

I nodded. "My granddaughter, Quinn, painted it, not that you can see much of it through the mud right now. She's quite the artist. You've probably seen her around town. She's the groundskeeper for Paisley Pointe. I'll introduce you sometime."

While we were talking, Harvey was sneaking up on Jack's work boots. He got a good grip on one of the laces and tugged.

"What in the world?!?" Jack exclaimed, taking a step back. "How'd these ducks get in here?" Harvey was following him, trying to grab the lace again.

I laughed. "You *are* new around here. This is Peeper, and the one trying to steal your shoelaces is Harvey. They're quite the pair. They go almost everywhere with me."

Jack pointed at Harvey's droopy wing. "What happened to him?"

"Harvey was in the wrong place at the wrong time. He can't fly anymore, which is why he's with me."

Dusty came back inside and shook the water off his jacket. "You got lucky, Granny. The wheel is undamaged. I added a little air to the tire. You're good to go."

"Hey, Dusty. Did you know about these ducks, man? Ms. Appleton – I mean Granny – was just telling me about how this one can't fly. Speaking of flying," Jack smirked, "did you tell her about what you saw last night?"

"What happened, Dusty?"

Dusty looked confused for a second, then embarrassed. "Nah, she would be interested in no tomfoolery." He flapped his hand dismissively and headed back to the front counter. The water cooler gave a small glug.

Now I *had* to know. "Try me, Dusty. I'm interested in all sorts of things." I leaned forward and gave my most encouraging look. I was genuinely interested, and not just because I live in a small town where not much happens.

Jack chimed in, "Go on, tell her, Dusty. I want to hear the story again, too." His grin made Dusty squirm all the more.

Dusty rubbed one calloused hand over his face and took a deep breath. "Oh fiddlesticks! I'll tell you, but you've got to promise not to laugh." He shook his finger at Jack. "I never should've told you about it. I don't normally believe in this kind of stuff, but ..."

I was on the edge of my seat and the ducks were staring at him expectantly, too.

"Last night I got up around midnight to get a snack," Dusty said. He rubbed his large stomach. "I'm wasting away here, as you can tell. Have to keep up my strength, you know." He wiggled his eyebrows and smiled. Then he frowned and licked his lips. "I was standing at my kitchen sink, eating a bowl of cereal. I love those toasted oats with some banana sliced on top. You put a little sugar on them and they just hit the spot. Don't tell my wife, though. I'm supposed to be watching my calories. She thinks I might be getting pre-diabetic. But what does she know? She's just a nurse."

He grinned and picked up a ballpoint pen. After clicking it a few times, he continued. "Anyway, the lights were all off in the house and I was looking outside, staring at nothing, just wishing the rain away. I love the rain and all, but this storm is ridiculous with a capital R. Light rain is nice, good fishing when that happens. Now that the river is brown with mud, you can't even get a nibble. I'm standing there, just zoning out, thinking about the last fish I caught. All of a sudden, something with red lights on it streaks past the window!" He clapped his hands together and pushed one of them forward, demonstrating the speed of the object.

CHAPTER 3

"Like a reflection of taillights?" I asked.

Dusty shook his head. "No, my kitchen faces the back yard. It wasn't no taillights. There wasn't no sound, neither. Just a blur with red lights on it. It was freaky." His eyes were big and I could tell that he wasn't trying to pull my leg.

Jack laughed. "Dusty's convinced what he saw was a gen-u-ine UFO. Have you seen any aliens around town, Granny?"

"A UFO? Really, Dusty? You are the most down-to-earth person I know. You know there's no such thing."

"I told you I don't believe in those things, but I saw what I saw," Dusty said, slapping the counter next to him. The sudden noise made the ducks jump. "Whatever it was, it was flying. I've worked on lots of mechanical stuff in my life and I haven't never seen nothing like what was out there last night. It was going too fast for me to get a good look at it, but nothing about it was familiar." His eyebrows were all bunched up and he was pointing his beefy finger at Jack. I don't think I've ever seen such a stern look on Dusty's face.

Jack put his hands up and took a step back. "Hey, man. I believe you saw something. It's just that thinking you saw a UFO ... it cracks me up."

A crash came from behind the counter, followed by loud quacking. Harvey waddled quickly around the corner dragging a long blue wire attached to a small black box.

I caught the thief and wrestled the booty from his bill. Silently, I thanked Harvey for creating a diversion. The tension in the room was getting thick. Handing the electronic part to Jack, I said, "I'd best be letting the two of you get back to work. It was nice meeting you, Jack. Dusty, how much do I owe you for the tire service?"

Dusty's easy smile returned and he said, "It's on the house.

Thanks for dropping by, Granny. I hope you have a lovely day, madam." He held the door and escorted me to the golf cart, making sure the ducks and I were safely inside before returning to the shop.

I mulled over Dusty's experience as I delivered the rest of the eggs. He truly was one of the most level-headed, calm individuals I knew. Nothing ruffled his feathers, so to speak. Not even the time a skunk fell into the oil changing pit in his shop. He was just that kind of mellow soul who made everyone around him feel secure. To have Dusty Meadows that agitated about seeing something at night was a little disturbing. I shook my head. There had to be a logical explanation for what he saw.

Chapter 4

I made sure to turn the radio on in the kitchen while Quinn and I ate dinner. I didn't want to miss the winners of the day's drawings. Besides that, I enjoyed listening to the mix of old and new music WPLY played. Variety is the spice of life, you know. In music as well as wigs.

While we dug into fluffy piles of mashed potatoes, spicy green beans, and meatloaf, I told Quinn about the contest.

"That explains all the questions I got today," she said. "I had no idea what people were talking about. Did you put your name in the drawing?"

"I sure did! I put yours in as well. It would be good for you to get away on a vacation. You've been working way too hard lately." I mentally added, *"and avoiding dealing with your painful breakup."*

Quinn reached for the salt and pepper, looking everywhere but at me. "This weather's making things nuts. There's so much flooding out at the ball field that I may have to redo the entire infield."

The opening notes of the song "Walking on Sunshine" came out of the radio.

"This is it!" I exclaimed, rubbing my hands together. "This is the song they're using to announce the daily winners!" I don't know why I had butterflies in my stomach. It was just a bag of seeds and a sun visor, for crying out loud. I guess it was just the fact that something was breaking the monotony of the dreary gray days.

"We're setting a record for bonkers days, folks. This is Wally Teller, your weather feller. Before we get to the forecast, though, it's my duty and pleasure to announce today's contest winners." A snare drum sounded. "The five-pound bag of sunflower seeds from Paisley Farm and Feed goes to ... Laurie Dodson! Hey, Laurie, did you ever think about the fact that even if a bear wears socks and shoes, he still has bear feet? Haha!

"And the winner of the stylish sun visor from Dusty's Garage is ... Sid Foley! When I took my car to Dusty the other day, he asked me if I wanted the good news or the bad news. I told him I wanted the good news, of course. He told me that my glove compartment was in great condition. Haha!

"Congratulations to today's winners. You can redeem your prizes at the stores that donated them. Don't forget, folks, all is not lost. Even if you didn't win today, your entries will now be placed in the big pot for the grand prize weekend getaway to sunny Florida. Oh! And one more thing. The winner of the grand prize will be announced on Saturday night at our Bring Back the Sun Dance to be held in the high school gym at 7 o'clock. Be there or be square!"

Quinn and I looked at each other in surprise. A dance? How fun! What a great way to chase the blues away. Before my husband Chet passed away, we were regulars on the dance floor. I mentally went through my closet to see what I could wear.

"A dance? Really? Ugh. Couldn't they just announce the winner on the radio and be done with it?" Quinn asked. She stabbed her meatloaf with more force than necessary.

CHAPTER 4

I was shocked at her reaction. "What do you mean? It'll be fun. Good music, good food, good company," I said. "You could meet some people your own age. Make some new friends." Quinn had been isolating herself so much that it worried me. I know that her breakup had been painful, both personally and professionally. But I felt that enough time had passed that she should start being a little more social.

Quinn lifted the corners of her mouth slightly and put her hand over mine. I noticed that she had a few cuts and scratches from working on the water pump at the lake. "I know, I know, Granny. It's just been hard to make myself get out there. I'm not sure I'm ready yet. I want to find someone as special to me as Grandpa was to you."

Running my finger over one of the scratches, I said, "I'm not saying you should dive back into dating. Take your time with that, for heaven's sake. Just be social. Give yourself a break." I paused. "I met Dusty's new mechanic today, Jack. He's about your age. He would probably give you a hand with that troublesome machinery if you asked him."

Quinn pulled her hand from my grasp. Frowning, she said, "You didn't try to set me up on a date with him, did you?"

"Oh, no. I just mentioned your name to him. Maybe he'll be at the dance. He's really nice. I think you'll like him."

Taking her dishes to the sink, Quinn said, "Good. Please don't try to play matchmaker, Granny. I'm still trying to forget the disaster of a dinner we had with Offer Baird." She shuddered.

"How was I supposed to know he would show up with a fiancé?" I asked. "I had no idea that he was engaged."

"Just don't," Quinn said, throwing down the dishtowel and storming out of the room.

Chapter 5

Pushing my bedroom curtain aside, I looked out on another gloomy morning. The trees in the yard were droopy from the weight of wet leaves. The sound of raindrops on the window made me want to crawl back into bed and cover my head. But there were animals to feed and other chores to be done.

I went through the kitchen and grabbed my rain gear. Quinn came out of her room and joined me. Wags and Brock came off their beds to greet us. Wags stretched her short gray and black legs. Her barrel-shaped body barely cleared the floor while Brock towered over her wagging his thin brown tail slowly from side to side. He was mostly a German shepherd with an unknown other doner thrown into the mix. He looked up at me with his chocolate brown eyes, the iconic expressive eyebrows shifting up and down. I don't think they were ready to start their day, either.

Together, the four of us made our way to the tall red classic barn, holding each other up as we slipped and slid through the mud. Ducks and dogs performed their morning rituals of sniffing, quacking, and peeping at each other.

"Sorry about last night," Quinn murmured as she picked up a pitchfork and stabbed at the open bale of hay. "I know you have the best intentions. I'm just feeling ultra-sensitive right now.

Must be this darned rain."

I shrugged. "No harm done. I just want the best for you." I hugged her shoulders and headed down to the other end of the barn, passing the nook that she had turned into a mini art studio. She had set up an easel and a half-finished canvas perched on it.

Quinn and I had a system where we traded off chores each day. That way, neither of us got stuck always doing the harder ones and we got a break from the ones we didn't particularly enjoy.

Today, it was my turn to milk our cow, Pearl. She had earned the nickname 'Pearl the Pain' with good reason. She was a great milker but very particular about everything. Some would even say she was a diva. She was very skittish and the smallest sound would cause her to jump. If she didn't like the angle you were sitting at, she would turn and head-butt you.

I eased my way into her stall, talking to her in soothing tones. I carried a pan of oats with me, which sometimes did the trick, and gave her something to do while I worked. This morning, she would have nothing to do with me or the oats. She circled the pen and shook her head menacingly. As much as I wanted to argue with her, I knew it wouldn't do any good. You can't reason with a grumpy cow. What did work was a short piece of rope around her back leg secured to a ring on the wall, preventing her from kicking or turning on me. It didn't keep her from trying, though.

As I was lugging the milk pail into the kitchen, I heard, "This is Wally Teller, your weather feller, signing off." Quinn was standing at the stove, making scrambled eggs.

"Darn, I missed it," I said, setting the pail on the counter.

"Missed what?"

"The weather report." I arranged the straining equipment in the sink, clamping the cheesecloth to the frame.

"Just another rainy day," Quinn sighed. "You didn't miss anything."

I poured the rich, creamy milk through the strainer. "I figured as much. What I actually wanted to hear was the locations of today's giveaways."

"You're really getting into this contest, aren't you?"

"I'd like to give you a proper vacation somewhere nice," I told her, wrapping my arms around her shoulders and squeezing. "You are such a big help around here. I don't know how I ever managed without you."

"Well, in that case, you'd better go and visit True Colors and the library today."

We sat at the table together and said grace. "I needed to visit the hair salon anyway. I want Priscilla to freshen up one of my wigs to wear to the dance on Saturday."

After Quinn left for work, I went to my room and chose a short, dark-colored wig, settling it over my thinning gray hair. Checking the mirror, I pinched my cheeks to bring out some color. I may not look quite like Liza Minelli, but I felt a lot younger. Satisfied with my appearance, I donned my raincoat and boots.

With my bag safely secured in the back seat and the ducks in the front, we set off for town. As we approached the bridge over the Paisley River, I slowed. The light-colored stones were stacked like what I imagined you would find on a castle in the English countryside. The bridge sloped gently up one side of three graceful arches and down the other side to become Paisley Pointe's Main Street. Normally, the river was medium-sized, meandering slowly between its banks. It was just deep enough to swim in and had plenty of water for irrigating crops. Today, though, it was unrecognizable. Water that was usually crystal clear ran muddy and silty and lapped at the tops of the banks like it was looking for weak spots. It was much louder, too, no longer a musical backdrop to our beautiful valley. Too much more rain and we could have a real problem on our hands.

Dropping off the other side of the bridge, I drove down Main. I loved how unique our business district was. Paved with red bricks and curving all the way around Paisley Park, each of the tall historic stone buildings faced the manicured lawns and beautiful lake that was offset to one side. A heart-shaped island graced the center of the lake. It looked like a postcard picture to me. On a bright sunny day, the green from the old cottonwood trees and willows on the island reflected in the still waters while the wild ducks that lived there paddled around. I think that John Paisley, the explorer who founded our little community, would be quite proud.

Exiting Main onto Harp Street, I passed Doc Worthington's veterinary clinic. I made a mental note to stop in and get some of the special ointment that he prescribed for Pearl when her udder was looking dry and cracked.

I turned next door into our library's parking lot. Even though it didn't exactly blend with the grand stone architecture of Main Street, I liked the sprawling brick building. A lot of thought had gone into making it a comfortable, inviting place, accessible to everyone.

I made sure the ducks stayed in the golf cart, checking the snaps and zippers twice. They weren't too happy about being left behind and were very vocal about it. I didn't plan on staying very long. Ignoring their protests, I walked up the curving ramp to the wide front doors. Taped to the glass on one of the side panels was a large green poster with the words 'IT'S COMING' splashed across it in black. No other words on it anywhere.

I pulled open the door, pausing in the entry to sniff appreciatively at the smells of wood, paper, and ink, I thought that someone should bottle it and turn it into a perfume. I would wear it. I glanced around the space, taking in the children's wing, complete with bean bag chairs and a puppet theater on the left. To the right was the adult section with computer stations, small tables, and comfy reading chairs grouped invitingly around a fireplace.

Right in the center was the circulation desk – a half circle with a dark granite countertop with three computer stations. The obligatory book return slot was located off-center to the right in the maple veneer. Standing behind the desk looking at me over reading glasses was the head librarian, and my good friend, Willa Mansfield. Willa and I had met shortly after I married Chet and moved to the farm. A lifelong bond had formed quickly and was as strong today as it was when we were a foursome instead of a pair of widows.

Willa moved out from behind the desk to give me a hug. "How are you doing today, darling?" she said, squeezing me against her ample bosom. She smelled faintly of cigarette smoke and coffee. She pulled the glasses off her face, revealing a network of fine laugh lines. Her cheeks were round and plump and her short gray hair made her look a little like Mrs. Claus.

"Nothing to complain about," I answered, returning the hug. "How's your hip doing with all this rain?"

"Achy, but nothing I can't handle." Willa rubbed the well-padded, offending area.

"What's with the cryptic poster on the front doors?" I asked, jabbing my thumb over my shoulder.

"Oh, that," she waved a dismissive hand. "Some alien watch group asked if they could hang it." She snapped her fingers. "I just remembered something I wanted to show you. Are you in a hurry?" Without waiting for my response, she turned on her heel and motioned me to follow her to her office. "I was reading some online periodicals yesterday and ran across an interesting article in the entertainment section of the *Manhattenier*. Have you seen it?"

She turned sideways and maneuvered herself into her office chair. The office was small and cramped. The two chairs on the opposite side of the desk were covered with books waiting to be cataloged and shelved. A couple of boxes were stacked next to the door. On the walls were some old photos of Paisley Pointe from when it was first founded as well as a map of the county. I set my bag down next to a large bookcase overflowing with papers and books and stood next to her as she clicked through the 50 or so open tabs on her browser. Navigating internet sites, in general, gave me heart palpations. Watching her move rapidly around the screen made me feel sick to my stomach. How did she know how to do that?

"Aha! Here it is." Triumphantly, she turned the monitor so that I was face-on with it. The article's title stood out in bold print at the top of the page: UP-AND-COMING ARTIST BRINGS HIGH PRICE FOR GALLERY. Directly under this was a lovely headshot of ... Quinn?

I turned to Willa, not understanding what I was looking at.

"Just when were you going to tell me that your granddaughter was in the paper?" Willa asked. "And that she was the talk of New York City?" She gave me that look over her reading glasses. You know the one. The teacher look.

"When was this article published?" I searched the page for a date. Quinn hadn't said anything to me about having a showing.

Willa leaned back in her chair, which squeaked under protest.

"This was Sunday's paper." She was giving me the stink-eye.

Straightening up, I said, "I don't know anything about this. Quinn would have told me about it, I'm sure. Is this a recent exhibition? Maybe they were having a slow news day and were rehashing something from the past."

"Nope. The article says that the show just closed on Saturday." Willa reached for the mouse and clicked. A soft whirring sound came from behind her. She grabbed the sheets of paper as they came from the printer. "Take it home with you. Ask Quinn what's going on. And then tell me. I'm dying to know!"

In light of the bombshell that Willa had just dropped on me, it would be logical for me to rush out and find Quinn right then, wouldn't it? But I needed some time to figure out just how to broach the topic, and I think better when I'm baking. Which led to why I was in the library in the first place.

Half dazed, I took the sheaf of papers and laid them gently on the bottom of my bag, taking out the cookbook I had brought back. "I'll do that," I said. "In the meantime, do you have any more cookbooks with pie recipes? This one doesn't have exactly what I'm looking for."

Willa gave a throaty laugh, showing her crooked teeth. "Still trying to find that perfect one, are we? Let's go look." She led the way to the non-fiction stacks. "Here you go, Irma. Have you looked into the series published by that internet chef? You know, the one who goes all over the world trying foods and then recreating them with an American flair? I think you'd really like those. We don't have them, but I've been contemplating ordering them. Do you suppose there would be an interest in something like that?" She paused to take a breath.

"Excuse me, Ms. Mansfield," a young woman said, standing at the end of the shelving. "There's a call for you. I think it's that distributor you've been wanting to talk to." She bobbed her head and backed away.

Willa rolled her eyes and said, "Well, duty calls. Some of these distributors are such a pain in the neck. They have no understanding of deadlines and budgets." She walked away, still talking.

As her voice faded, I picked up a book and smiled to myself. Willa never changed. I wondered what it was like in the evenings at her house. Did she ever run out of words? Maybe that's what drew her to library work. She was always surrounded by them. I'd bet money that she even talked in her sleep.

Now that I was alone, I could focus. The library was quiet, but not silent. I could hear folks' fingers clicking on keyboards, muffled conversations, and pages turning. It was peaceful and calming.

I browsed for a while. I wasn't sure what I was looking for, I just knew that I'd know it when I saw it. After years of making pies, I wanted a challenge. Something new and different. Like the zucchini pie that I'd made for Chief Ellis a few weeks ago. That recipe had been in one of my magazines. If I couldn't find a unique recipe, I would just have to invent my own, I decided. After searching for several more minutes, I settled on a collection of recipes published by a popular women's magazine. The title claimed that they were 'award-winning concoctions'. Having won several local baking contests myself, I had pretty high expectations.

I wandered back toward the circulation desk and spotted a tuft of bright green hair above one of the computer dividers. Shaking my head at the strange sight, I turned to the yellow box with its hopeful message sitting on a table near the door. I had forgotten that was one of the reasons for coming to the library.

Willa was on the phone, so I crossed the floor and filled out a card. A placard next to the box showed the cover of a magazine called *Beach Getaways*. White sand and bright blue water dotted with sailboats filled the page. I looked up and glanced through the glass door at the sloppy, gloomy street, sighing. Just looking at that picture made it feel worse. I reached for a second card and put down Quinn's information, thinking, *if that article is true, she'll be able to afford to go somewhere very exotic, indeed!*

Spotting one of the assistant librarians, I went to the desk to check out the cookbook. Willa was still on the phone. She had taken a seat and was writing notes on a legal pad. That was fine with me. I didn't want to leave the ducks cooped up in the golf cart for too long.

I made it to the door just as a tall man in a long camel-colored trench coat came through. He stepped to the side and held it for me. I glanced up at him and said, "Thank you so much." Then I did a double take. "Isaiah? What are you doing here?"

"Can't a guy come and say hi to his favorite grandmother?" Isaiah flashed a wide, dimpled smile. His sculpted jaw was clean-shaven and his short dark hair glistened with raindrops. His gray eyes sparkled with amusement. "How are you, Granny? It's been a while."

I gave him a quick hug, noting that I only came up to his armpit. "Oh, you know, can't complain. Any day above ground is a good day. The real question is how are *you* doing?" I craned my neck to get a good look at him.

"Didn't Nanna tell you? I've moved back to Paisley Pointe and opened my own law office." His deep baritone voice was musical.

"We haven't had a chance to visit much lately," I said. I gestured back to the desk where Willa, phone to her ear, waved

CHAPTER 5

at us. "I've got to get going now. Will you be coming to the dance on Saturday night? Maybe we can catch up then?"

And maybe introduce you to Quinn, I thought as I trotted back out to the parking lot. The last time I'd seen Isaiah Strong he was a pimple-faced teenager, just getting ready to go off to college. I'd heard lots about him from Willa, of course, but I didn't realize what a hunk he'd turned out to be. And a lawyer to boot. Half of what she said I'd discounted as grandmotherly pride. Wouldn't it be something if my granddaughter and Willa's grandson became an item? I got chills just thinking about it.

I was still smelling his cologne on my jacket and daydreaming about their future relationship as I pulled out onto the street.

Chapter 6

The front right tire struck something and rolled over it, making a crunching noise and jostling me and the ducks, who were contentedly sleeping on the floorboards. They came awake suddenly, quacking, peeping, and flapping up a storm. Feathers flew in all directions in the confined space. Did I just find another pothole?

I fought the wheel as we skidded around. Just when I got the wheels straightened out, something big slammed into the back of the golf cart. My head hit the steering wheel and my wig slipped down to my nose.

Dazed, I sat there for a second. Then groans started coming from whoever had hit me. Casting a sideways glanced at the ducks to be sure they were OK, I put my wig to rights, wincing at the knot beginning to form on my forehead, and stepped out onto the rain-slicked street.

Bits of bent metal tubing and bright green strapping were strewn across the road. A skateboard lay overturned with its wheels still spinning. A pair of jeans-clad legs was moving behind the cart, so I stepped over the mess to see who it was.

I got to the back of the vehicle just as the person slowly sat up and took off the safety orange bicycle helmet that was perched on their head. They put their face in their hands. More loud

CHAPTER 6

groans spurred me to rush over and kneel beside them.

"Are you alright?" I asked. I put a hand on the sleeve of their oversized blue windbreaker and noticed that there was a huge rip in the material. "Looks like you've got some road rash there. Do I need to call an ambulance?" My voice was getting very high-pitched at this point.

The individual shook their head and then I saw the receding hairline. And the letters WPLY on the front of the jacket. "Wally? Wally Teller?"

Wally looked up at me with soulful eyes and straightened his glasses. "Yes, Granny, it's me. No, I don't require an ambulance, but I could use some help finding my other shoe." He squinted through the rain splotches on his lenses.

Looking down, I noticed his dirty white sock with one big toe poking through a hole.

"Oh! Of course!" I scrambled to my feet and scanned the ground. Another skateboard with more metal tubing attached to it was jammed halfway under the back of my cart. I spotted a black high-top tennis shoe mixed in with the carnage.

Extricating the shoe from a knot of green nylon rope that snaked its way under the golf cart, I handed Wally his footwear, then helped him to his feet. I was careful to avoid the scrape on his arm and another on the palm of his hand.

By this time, we were both soaking wet and shivering. Wally limped around picking up pieces. I unzipped one side of the cart and said, "Put them in here, Wally, and then I'll take you home."

He nodded silently and placed the crushed whatever-it-was in the back seat. I rounded up the two skateboards and added them to the pile. Wally pulled on the green rope and groaned as a mangled mess came out from underneath the vehicle.

"Oh, man! My RC car is toast." He gently picked up the toy

car and cradled it in his arms like a baby.

Not knowing what else to do, I guided him to the front seat and helped him onto it, shooing the ducks to the floor. Climbing in next to Wally, I said, "Which way to your house?"

Wiping the water from his face, Wally said, "Corner of Hill View and Conway Rise. Blue house on the right." He stared mournfully at the wreck in his arms. Was he crying or was that rain on his face?

Looking around carefully – not making that mistake again – I made a U-turn and headed to Wally's house.

The big pine trees out front almost obscured the cute little bungalow where Wally lived. He directed me around the side to where a small detached garage was located. The house and garage reminded me of robin's eggs with white trim. There wasn't much grass to speak of but the yard was freshly raked.

I parked in front of the garage. Wally limped to the side door, unlocked it, and activated the large wooden overhead door.

I carried a pile of twisted metal into what I would call controlled chaos. We unloaded all of the scraps and pieces from the wreck and piled them in a corner near a long workbench covered with wires, screws, tools, and electrical tape.

As I was setting the skateboards down, I heard quacking. Harvey and Peeper, obviously tired of the cramped quarters, had managed to wiggle their way out of the cart and joined us in the garage. They wandered around, examining everything while shaking their tail feathers. My interest was piqued, too. I knew that Wally liked to tinker, but had no idea about the extent of his hobby. There were half-assembled radios, tires of various sizes, and old coffee cans filled to the brim with nails and screws. Every horizontal surface was covered with one project or another.

"Come back here with that!" Wally yelled. I turned just in

CHAPTER 6

time to see Harvey, trailing a long red wire, waddling as fast as his little legs could carry him out into the rain. Peeper was behind him, trying to keep up, and behind her limped poor Wally. Unfortunately for him, Peeper's webbed feet got tangled in Harvey's wire, causing her to tumble, bill over tail feathers, into a bucket of round ball bearings. The crash was deafening. Wally couldn't stop in time and tripped over her, landing face-first in a puddle of what looked to me like oil.

Wally spluttered and coughed and stood slowly to his feet. He attempted to wipe the mess off, with little effect. He took a couple of steps and winced.

"Let's get you cleaned up and doctored in the house," I said. Wally leaned on me as we made our way to the door. Calling the ducks, I shut the large overhead door and then the side one after everyone was out.

Large cement circles marked the path to the small porch at the back of the house. Harvey and Peeper followed sedately behind us. It was almost as if they understood that they had done something wrong.

Inside the house, it was another story. It was like turning a child loose in a candy store. Harvey and Peeper took off in separate directions, making all sorts of noise. I had to choose between chasing after them or helping poor Wally.

I chose Wally, feeling horrible that my distracted driving had caused the accident. I just hoped that the ducks would behave themselves.

I pulled out a kitchen chair for Wally. He sat heavily and leaned forward with his head in his hands. I left him there as I went in search of a bathroom, returning a few minutes later with a wet washcloth, antiseptic, and bandages. He was well-stocked for clumsy accidents. I also picked up a fresh shirt for him from the pile on his bed.

Wally's housekeeping skills were impressive. It was obvious that he lived alone, but there was surprisingly little mess for being a bachelor pad. I didn't have to clear away any empty beer bottles or pizza boxes to make room on the small kitchen table. I even spotted an African violet blooming on the windowsill over the sink.

The only place that was in disarray was the dining room table. It, like the workbenches in the garage, was covered with wires and switches and fancy little light bulbs. Of course, this area drew Harvey like a magnet. He was spreading his lopsided wings and hopping, trying to reach some yellow wires that were hanging over the edge.

As I dabbed antiseptic cream on Wally's elbow, I asked, "What was that ... contraption you had out on the street?" I wanted to say 'hunk of junk', but stopped myself just in time. I wasn't in any position to be judgmental of him or his gadgets.

Wally winced. "Ouch, that stings!" He blew out his breath and pushed his glasses up. "That was a new prototype of a mobility device." He tried to bend his elbow and inspect the damage.

"You mean wheelchair?"

"I guess you could call it that," Wally shrugged. "I call it a scooter cycle."

"I think you should go back to the drawing board," I said gently, placing a bandage over the raw skin on his arm.

Out of the corner of my eye, I saw Harvey, who had given up on reaching the yellow wire, busily working on tugging something thin and flat out of a black backpack that had been left on the floor. Wally started to turn his head in that direction. I stood up quickly and blocked his view. "Well, you should probably take some painkillers and lie down for a while, Wally." I helped him to the couch and found a pillow for his head. Bringing a bottle of pills from the bathroom, I set it and a glass of water on the coffee table within easy reach. I put the TV remote next to the glass. "We'll show ourselves out. I'm so sorry we ran into each other like that."

"Hey, Granny?"

"Yes?"

"Why do seagulls fly over the sea?"

"What are you talking about?"

"Because if they flew over the bay, they'd be bagels. You know, like lox and bagels?"

I turned my head away before he caught my eye roll. "Goodbye, Wally. Rest up."

Walking quickly to the kitchen, I saw that Harvey had almost worked the object out of the bag. It looked like one of those snap bracelets that stay flat until you tap it on your wrist to make it wrap around. I pushed it back into the pack and scooped Harvey under my arm, calling for Peeper.

Back in the golf cart, I scolded the two rascals. "We all need to be more careful and watch where we put our noses from now on. And mind our manners when we are guests in someone's home." In response, all I got was nuzzles.

Chapter 7

Harvey and Peeper agreed to be more careful in the future. At least I hope they did. I was feeling so frazzled that I forgot where I was supposed to go next. Reaching under my wig, I pulled out the list and unfolded it. No deliveries to make today, just the library and the hair salon.

The hair salon! The dance! My own hair was hopeless, but I knew Priscilla would work a miracle on my wig. Not the one I was wearing, which I was sure was a mess, too.

After checking both ways – twice – I pulled slowly onto the residential street and headed back toward the business district. I saw two women walking down the street toward me with the same bright green hair I had just seen in the library. They were dressed in what looked to me like those blue flight suits that pilots wear in the military. What was going on around town? I knew that Priscilla knew everything that happened in Paisley Pointe and I couldn't wait to ask her.

True Colors Hair Salon was located in one of the historic downtown buildings. It had giant plate-glass windows and a prime corner location. I pulled up in front of the shop and let the ducks lead the way to the door. Even in the current overcast conditions, Priscilla's shop was warm and inviting. The vibrant yellow walls and oversized posters of outrageous hairstyles gave the place a cheerful feeling.

The shop's owner was even more cheerful. Her vintage outfit, a white poodle skirt covered with cherries with a short-sleeved sweater set was the perfect match to her red lipstick and nail polish. With her blonde beehive hairdo, she truly could have stepped out of a 1954 Life Magazine.

"Good morning, Granny," Priscilla called from the shampoo bowl in the back of the shop. "Good morning, my widdle wuvs." The ducks didn't seem to mind her baby talk. "Make yourselves comfy, darlings. I'll be just a minute."

I found a chair by the window and sat down. The ducks, however, went exploring. Harvey seemed to feel that it was his duty to find every lost bobby pin and hair tie when we visited. Peeper was more interested in nibbling on Priscilla's bright red toenails. She was used to it and acted like it was an everyday occurrence to have waterfowl underfoot in her shop. In fact, she had started keeping a small jar of treats for the ducks.

Soon, she shut off the water and brought her client back to the styling chair closest to the waiting area. When the towel came off, I caught a glimpse of who it was.

"Hello, Laurie," I said. "Fancy seeing you here." Laurie Dodson was married to Chris Dodson, the dairyman I had run into yesterday at the feed store. She and Chris had four small children, but she still found the time to run the children's programs at our church. It seemed that the only place we ever saw each other, outside of Sundays, was here or at the library. Life on a farm is a 24/7 proposition and there isn't much time for luxuries like spa days.

Laurie smiled. I had always been jealous of her cute heart-shaped face and full lips. "Good to see you, Granny. How are things at your farm? Being so close to the river, I imagine you're dealing with the same flooding issues we are. I know we're keeping a close eye on it. Chris is starting to get very worried. The bend in the river on our property is starting to catch some bigger branches and stuff."

"Can't complain," I said. "Having the house and barnyard on a small rise is definitely a blessing. The river is still holding to its banks, but not for long, I'm afraid. Congratulations on winning yesterday's drawing, by the way."

Laurie frowned. "I won? Really? This is the first I've heard of it."

"They announced your name on the radio last night," Priscilla said, snapping her gum. She pulled back a section of hair and snipped. "You won the five-pound sack of sunflower seeds."

"Chris and I were busy helping one of our cows birth a large calf last night. We didn't make it inside until after ten o'clock."

Priscilla gasped. "Oh! Poor thing. Is it OK?" She paused with her scissors in the air. Her long fake eyelashes emphasized her wide eyes.

Laurie nodded. "Everyone is doing fine this morning. I wasn't so sure last night, though. I thought we were going to have to call Doc Worthington. Both mother and baby are right as rain today."

All three of us turned to look out the window. I laughed. "That's a funny way to put it, especially right now." Harvey and Peeper joined in our laughter.

"Chris will be so excited about those seeds. He loves eating them during baseball season. Hopefully, we get to have one this year."

Priscilla took the cape off Laurie's shoulders and picked up her broom. "Don't forget to put your name in today's drawing. I'm giving away a cute beach towel and suntan lotion." She gestured to the coffee table where the big yellow box sat on display.

"Your turn, Granny. What can I do for you today?" Priscilla propped the broom in the corner and turned to me. She squinted her eyes and leaned forward. "Wait. What happened to you?" She pointed a long red fingernail at my forehead.

Reaching up, I felt the goose egg that had formed there. "Just an unfortunate accident. It's nothing." Not wanting to become fodder for the gossip mill, I changed the subject. "What's with all the green hair I've been seeing? Is there some kind of new craze going around?"

"I've been seeing them, too. I didn't have anything to do with that, I swear. I would never dye a client's hair that icky color." She shuddered. "They just started showing up today. I'm not sure who they are, but I *will* find out."

"They are dressed strange, too." Laurie nodded.

I zipped open my bag and took out a blonde wig. "I call this one my Dolly Parton wig. But right now, it looks less Dolly and more 'Pardon the mess'. One of the cats thought it would be fun to play with," I said. "Do you think you could fix it? I want to wear it to the dance on Saturday."

Priscilla rotated the wig and looked at it closely. "No problem. I can make it look fabulous. You'll be the belle of the ball."

The door opened and Isla Marsh rushed in, closing her bright pink umbrella behind her. I hadn't seen her since the archery competition a few weeks ago. Her round gold-framed glasses were spotted with rain. Her short blonde hair was caught up in two tiny ponytails that stuck out on either side of her head. The oversized tie-dyed t-shirt over her jeans made her look like a child. She was muttering to herself as she took off her jacket and hung it on the coat tree by the door. Then I noticed that she had on one yellow rain boot and one pink one.

"Hello, Isla," we all chimed.

"Baby powder, diapers, bottle brush," Isla said. She looked up and her body jerked. "Oh! Hi everyone. Sorry. I forgot paper and need to remember to get some items at the store after my appointment. I thought if I kept repeating them, I won't forget. I have such a bad memory."

Priscilla walked over to the counter and picked up a pad of sticky notes and a pen. "Here you go, sweetie."

Isla sat down and wrote out her list. "Thank you so much. My neighbor had her baby a few days ago and they asked me to pick up some stuff for them. Betsy's mom is in town to help, but it seems like she is making more work, not less."

"Betsy Rollins? She's not due until next month." Priscilla glanced at the calendar on the wall.

"I know. It caught everyone off guard. Hence the trip to the store. They are scrambling to get stuff set up because they thought they had all this time." Isla tucked the note into her pocket and handed the pen back.

I stood up and called for the ducks. "Well, sounds like I should head over and see what I can do to help out. Having a baby is stressful enough without being unprepared on top of it." I hurried to the golf cart and got everyone situated. Checking the time on the bank across the street, I saw that it was getting close to lunchtime, so I went to Manuel's Market to pick up a few ingredients for lunch and a pie recipe from the cookbook I'd just gotten at the library. It would be the perfect one to take to Betsy this afternoon.

Chapter 8

I packed the mini peanut butter pies into a large plastic container, tickled about how they had turned out. The chocolate pie dough was cut with a flower-shaped cookie cutter and baked in mini muffin tins. The cream filling was light and fluffy and the chocolate drizzle put them over the top. Quinn and I each had one with our lunch – for quality assurance, of course. I figured they were just about perfect to take to a new mother. Being bite-sized, they could be eaten with one hand and didn't dirty any dishes.

As I put the dessert in the golf cart, Harvey and Peeper came running. Peeper had her snow-white wings spread wide as she approached the vehicle. Harvey was trying, unsuccessfully, to copy her. He reminded me of a kid brother attempting to keep up with an older sibling.

"Not this time, guys," I said. "Brand new mommies aren't appreciative of having ducks in their house. You'll have to sit this one out." I shook a pan of cracked corn and led them to the barn. I closed them in, feeling only slightly guilty. After all, they had already been to town with me once today.

I admired the stately architecture of the older homes in Isla and Betsy's neighborhood. Big old trees with bright green leaves stood guard on every lawn. Hedges lined the walkways and nearly every house had a porch. To me, a porch is the equivalent of a smile on a house.

Seeing a familiar rusty camper van driving right at me, going way too fast, I pulled quickly to the curb. I watched as it passed me and saw bright green hair again. On the side of the vehicle were hand-painted letters. I was able to make out two giant purple Ps before it sped away.

Betsy's porch was wide and comfortable, with white rocking chairs and side tables filled with brightly colored potted flowers. Climbing the steps, I imagined spending summer afternoons sitting out there with a glass of iced tea and a good book. I twisted the old-fashioned doorbell in the middle of the sunny yellow door and admired the wreath made of burlap and ribbon hanging on it.

The rain pattered softly on the roof of the covered porch, but I was much more tuned in to the sounds from inside the house. I was hoping that I hadn't come when everyone was napping.

Running footsteps on creaky wooden floors approached the door, followed by slower heavier ones. The door opened a crack and a small tow-headed face appeared. "Dad! There's a lady out here!" It opened wider and I smiled at Betsy's husband, Felix. His black hair was disheveled and there were circles under his eyes. The dark beard he was wearing had passed the five o'clock shadow phase and was heading into northern woodsman territory.

"Granny!" Felix exclaimed brightly. "Come on in! Alex, you remember Granny, don't you?" He pulled me into a giant one-handed bear hug. I could see a woman hovering in the background with a sour look on her face. Her designer clothes looked out of place next to Felix's soft jeans and t-shirt.

I handed him my container and stepped inside, taking off my

boots and raincoat. I put them on the conveniently located hall tree.

"I won't stay long, Felix. I just wanted to come by and say congratulations on your new little one and maybe get to hold him for a minute." Turning to the woman, who was now wringing her professionally manicured hands, I introduced myself. "Hello. I'm Irma Appleton." The woman lifted her chin so that her gaze slid down her nose at me.

Felix handed back my container as Alex ran into the next room. "Granny, this is Betsy's mother, Roxanne Mathers. She is staying with us for a while. Mother, this is Granny Appleton, one of Paisley Point's sweetest residents."

"Very nice to meet you, Roxanne. How wonderful that you were able to come and help with the baby." I put as much sugar as I could muster on the greeting, which wasn't much.

Felix led the way into what would have been called the ladies' parlor in Victorian times. Betsy was sitting on the far corner of a couch upholstered in a fabric covered with cabbage roses. The wall behind her was the same mauve color as the roses. Under the lace-covered window, Alex sat in front of his toy box, playing.

"Hello, Betsy," I said softly. She was burping her tiny newborn. Her brown hair was caught up in a messy bun. She wore no makeup but had a natural glow about her. There were dark circles under her eyes, though, and they darted from Felix to her mother and back again.

I walked over to her, intending to sit on the couch, but Roxanne scooted ahead of me and sat right next to Betsy. I ignored her power play and sat on the matching armchair next to the sofa. "Congratulations! This is quite a surprise. Your little one just couldn't wait to see the world, could he?"

Before Betsy could even open her mouth to reply, her mother said, "It was a difficult birth. She has such a small build. Betsy was a trooper, though. She takes after me. Good pioneer stock, you know." Roxanne fussed over the blanket covering the baby and tucked in the edges.

Alex appeared at my elbow. "Want to see what my Nanna brought me?" Without waiting for my reply, he shoved a large plastic disc under my nose.

"It's a flying saucer!" he exclaimed. "It really works, too. Watch this!" Alex put the Frisbee-sized toy on the coffee table and operated a black remote control. Red lights came on around the perimeter of the saucer. A whirring noise started as the toy rose up off of the table and started circling the room. The craft wobbled and spun and bounced off the wall. Changing direction, it started coming straight at me. Felix stood up and grabbed it out of the air.

"I think that's enough, Alex," he said firmly. "Let's stick to flying this outside. We don't want to hit our guests."

"Oh, let the boy have his fun, Felix." Roxanne looked like the Cheshire cat. I think she would have cheered, had the spaceship smacked me in the head. "Since Felix is bound and determined to enter those silly drone races in Chicago again this year, I thought little Alex here should have his own. That way they can do some bonding when Felix practices."

Felix brought his lips into a tight line and shook his head at Alex. "We'll play with it later, OK?"

Alex looked at his dad, then his grandmother, then back to his dad. He took the toy from Felix and ran out of the room.

Clearing my throat and taking the lid off my container, I said, "I brought you a little treat to celebrate." The smells of chocolate and peanut butter wafted through the room.

Roxanne jumped up. "I see you failed to bring any napkins. I'll get some from the kitchen." With a stiff back, she left the room. Both Felix and Betsy visibly relaxed.

"Would you like to hold the baby?" Betsy asked with a small smile.

"You know I would," I said, coming over and taking Roxanne's coveted spot. Soon the tiny bundle of warmth and cuteness was nestled in my arms. As I gazed at the dark hair and tiny eyelashes brushing pink cheeks, my heart melted. "What's his name?" I asked, my voice barely above a whisper.

"We named him after my grandfather, Lucas," Felix said, sitting up a little straighter.

"Oh, how nice. Sharing a name with a loved one is a great way to give a child roots."

I pretended not to notice Betsy covering a yawn. "How are you holding up, Betsy? Lucas came a little earlier than you expected." As I was talking, Roxanne returned with a serving tray bearing a pitcher of iced tea, glasses, small plates, napkins, and forks. She paused and set her lips in a thin line when she saw me on the couch.

The smile on Betsy's face faded a little. "It's been kinda rough. Lucas has a very healthy appetite, so we are up every few hours."

"If you would bottle feed him as I told you to, other people could help you," Roxanne scolded. She handed me a glass that was less than half full of tea. It brought to mind the courting candles fathers used to use. They would set the height of the candle to determine the length of time the gentleman caller was allowed to stay. If they liked the suitor, the candle was longer. I had definitely been given a short candle.

Saluting Roxanne with my glass, I said, "Thank you. I purposely brought these finger desserts so that they won't make more work around here." I leaned forward to put my glass on a coaster, picked up one of the small sweets, and took a bite. The filling was light and creamy, the shell slightly crunchy and chocolaty – the perfect combination. It tasted a lot like a peanut butter cup. The best part, though, was the look on Roxanne's face as she warred between being the perfect hostess and putting me in my place.

Both Felix and Betsy followed my lead, picking up one of the snacks. "These are amazing!" Betsy gushed. "So rich and yet so light. Granny, you are a genius." She finished hers and picked up a second one.

Felix ate three in quick succession and downed a glass of tea. Roxanne just sat on the edge of her chair, holding her glass in one hand and crumpling a napkin in the other.

"You said that Lucas is a good eater?" I asked. "He seems to be very contented." I gazed down at the sleeping baby in my arms, instinctively rocking back and forth.

Betsy nodded. "Oh, yes. He's SO good. We are still figuring out the nighttime feeding thing, though. It seems that he sleeps more during the day. It's about every two hours that I have to be up with him." She rubbed her eyes. "Last night was super rough. Not because of him, though. I just couldn't sleep." She shuddered.

"She had all of us up," Roxanne complained. "Some cockamamie story about seeing a UFO. She's sleep-deprived. No wonder she's seeing things." She waved her hand dismissively.

Betsy looked down at her hands and blushed. "Mom, I didn't make that up. I saw something."

Was it just me, or did the temperature in the room just plummet? "A UFO?" I asked. "What did it look like?"

"It was a string of white lights going across the sky. I was

CHAPTER 8

sitting in the rocking chair in the nursery, looking out the window. These lights appeared. There were about four of them, all lined up in a row like they were playing follow the leader." Betsy's eyes were big. She used her hand to show the path of the lights.

"I'm going to have to agree with your mother on this one, Betsy," I said. "It was probably some headlights reflecting in the rain or something. When we're really tired, our brains can play tricks on us. Speaking of which, I think I should take my leave and you should get a nap in while young Lucas here is sleeping." Gently transferring the infant back to her, I stood up and held out my hand to Roxanne. All I got in return was a limp grip.

"It was nice to meet you, Roxanne. Felix, Betsy, congratulations on the new addition. If you need anything at all, you know where to find me."

Felix stood and walked me to the door while Roxanne helped Betsy to her bedroom to lie down.

"Thanks for stopping by," Felix said, "And for the great little pies." He lowered his voice. "I'm a little worried about Betsy. She's really upset about what she saw last night. I told her it was probably me, practicing night flying with my drone. It's my weakest area of competition. Plus it gives me some alone time if you know what I mean. She didn't believe me. She's convinced there are aliens in Paisley Pointe."

Laughing, I put a hand on his arm. "She'll come around after she gets some rest. Hallucinations are a part of sleep deprivation. You should go get some rest, too. You've been having to play referee as well as being dad and husband, I'll wager." I waggled my eyebrows at him. The image of a green haired man driving down this very street popped into my head, but I didn't share that with Felix.

Chapter 9

"Wally Teller, your weather feller, here with the winners of today's drawings." I had the radio volume up when they started to play "Walking on Sunshine" so I could hear it over the food processor. I was cutting shortening and butter into some flour to make pie crusts, but I didn't want to miss the announcement.

"Drum roll, please." A snare drum sounded. "The winner of the beach towel and suntan lotion donated by True Colors Hair Salon is ... Vivian Ellis. That will be perfect for lying outside with a book. I'm reading an anti-gravity book right now. It's so good, I can't put it down! Haha!

"The subscription to *Beach Getaways* magazine goes to ... Barbara Hodges. Hey, Barbara, do you know what the ocean said to the beach? Nothing. It just waved! Haha! Maybe looking at pictures of hot, sunny beaches will take your mind off the rain.

"Enjoy your prizes, ladies. You can collect them from the donating locations. The remaining entries will go into the big pot for the weekend getaway drawing to be held on Saturday night at the dance. See you there. This is Wally Teller, your weather feller, signing off."

I turned the radio off and dumped the pie dough onto the counter, not overly disappointed that I hadn't won. It was enough for me to get to socialize with my friends and participate in the excitement. If I won, I would probably give away my prize anyway. What would I do with suntan lotion? I couldn't see myself lying around somewhere doing nothing, trying to get a tan. Who has time for that?

Quinn came wandering into the kitchen from the living room. "Do you have any more of those peanut butter thingies?" she asked, reaching into the fridge for a glass of milk.

I pointed with my nose since my hands were covered with globs of dough. "In that container over there."

She helped herself to one and took a bite. "These are fabulous, by the way. Where did you get the recipe?" She finished that one and reached for another.

"I went to the library today and borrowed a new cookbook." A lightbulb went off in my head. In all the excitement that happened after I left the library, I had forgotten what I had learned about Quinn. The shock I had felt when I first saw the article came rushing back. I tried to look nonchalant, but my heart started racing. "Willa found an interesting article. She gave me a printout so I could show you. It's in my bag in the laundry room."

I continued to roll out the dough with one ear cocked toward the next room. I could hear the zipper being pulled and the rustle of papers coming out. Then silence. And more silence. It wasn't that big of an article. What was taking her so long?

Finally, Quinn came back into the kitchen. She was wearing the same expression I had when I first saw the headline and photo. "What is all this?" she asked, sitting down at the table.

"I was going to ask you the same thing. You didn't know about it?"

"No," she said slowly, her eyes glued to the page. "But it does

CHAPTER 9

explain the strange email I got yesterday. I thought it was one of those scams where you won a prize, but you have to pay for the shipping and stuff." She stood up and walked to her bedroom, returning with her laptop.

"Here it is," she said. "It's from LuxArt Galleries, where I had my last event." She read the email aloud. "Congratulations on a magnificent showing. We are thrilled with the response to your art and excited to work with you in the future. Our courier is standing by to deliver your compensation. Please provide a physical address and be prepared to produce your ID for confirmation purposes."

"I didn't know you had a showing."

Quinn laughed. "Neither did I."

Chapter 10

A crash of thunder was my wake-up call on Wednesday. Would this storm never end? Was it going to rain for 40 days and 40 nights like it did for Noah? I was beginning to think that maybe we should look into how much lumber it would take to build an ark. The gray-tinted light made me wonder if this was what it would look like to live underwater.

At the barn, Peeper and Harvey rushed out to greet the day. The other animals just looked at me like I was crazy. Pearl, the milk cow, was in a particularly sour mood. I had just gotten settled in when she kicked the leg of the milking stool and I found myself sitting on my tush in the straw. "Pearl, I get it. You're grumpy. I'm grumpy, too. But having a full bag is going to make you even grumpier. Please let me help you. Your calf can't possibly drink all that milk." I spent some time patting her head, scratching the root of her tail, and talking to her. I eased myself back into position and got knocked on my tailbone again.

Sighing, I said, "We can do this the easy way, or the hard way, Pearl. Your choice." I started to reach for the short rope I used to hold her kicking leg back. Then I remembered the small hand-held radio in the tack room. WPLY was playing oldies but goodies at this time of the morning. I turned it on and adjusted

CHAPTER 10

the volume.

Placing the radio on the ground next to me, I cautiously sat back down and placed the milk pail under Pearl. She swished her tail but stood still. I patted her copper and white colored side and rubbed her belly, then slid my hand down to her udder and started squeezing. She turned her head and nuzzled my shoulder, shifting her weight and relaxing one hip. Huh. I guess music really does soothe the savage beast.

Before long, I was singing along with the radio and squirting milk in time to the beat. Pearl was chewing her cud and ignoring me. Perfect. Then the music stopped.

"Good morning, Paisley Pointe. This is Wally Teller, your weather feller, here with today's forecast. We'll have to wear our rain gear for at least another few days, folks. This storm is a doozy! I've never seen anything like it. The low has decided to camp out right over us and pitch its tent, metaphorically speaking. I wouldn't be surprised if this one breaks some kind of record. Sorry to disappoint you.

"But here's the good news. You can head over to the recreation center and sign up for a prize today. Manuel's Market has a giveaway, too. That should brighten your day a little. Oh! Did you hear about the claustrophobic astronaut? He just wanted a little more space! Haha! This is Wally Teller, your weather feller, signing off."

Pearl turned her head and nudged my shoulder again. I patted her nose. "You want me to put your name in the drawing, Pearl? I'm not sure what they're giving away, but I don't think you would have any use for it." I stood up and moved the heavy pail. "I left plenty for Petey, don't you worry," I said, opening the connecting door to the next stall. Petey, a carbon copy of his mother's coppery brown and white splotches, was eager for his breakfast and wasted no time getting to it. I stood and watched him stamp his knobby-kneed legs and swish his little tail for a minute. My stomach growled and I headed back to the house for my own breakfast.

Chapter 11

I lingered over my cup of coffee, not really wanting to go back out in the rain. I wrote out a grocery list and tucked it securely under my sassy gray wig. Today's hairstyle included short, straight sides and back with spikes covering the top. I wasn't sure how it would fare with the wet conditions, but I was willing to risk it.

Arming myself with boots and a jacket, I let myself out the back door. Hearing the familiar squeak of the screen door, Harvey and Peeper came running. They were covered from head to tail feathers in mud. Harvey quacked up a storm as he settled on the floorboards. Peeper hopped in and peeped happily. "I'd give you two a bath, but you'd be back to looking like mud wrestlers in no time at all," I chuckled.

As the wipers did their best to keep up with the rain, I peered through the windshield at what used to be a dirt road. The county crew was going to have a heck of a time repairing all the damage when we finally dried out. In places, standing water covered the entire surface of the road. I drove slowly so we didn't get splashed as much. Approaching the Paisley River bridge, something caught my eye. It was a branch with leaves on it, floating downstream. Then I spied another one, and then a third. I couldn't believe how much debris was coming down the muddy river. There were plenty of small sticks and dried corn husks mixed in with the larger stuff, too. I was concerned that the detritus would get caught as it went between the bridge supports, so I stayed to watch for a few minutes. The larger chunks swirled a bit but eventually popped out on the other side. That was a relief. If things got worse, the floating objects could create a dam. Feeling better about things, I pressed the accelerator and bumped my way across the bridge.

The number of beat-up old cars on Main Street startled me. Normally, there were lots of cars, but these had a different feel to them. For one thing, they all sported the same bumper sticker. Bright purple letters spelled the words 'Perigee Prophets'. Whatever that means. These didn't belong to tourists bringing money to the shops that were giving off a cheerful glow from their windows, reflecting on the wet sidewalks. They seemed sinister, somehow.

I exited the circle and headed west to the edge of town where the big recreation center was perched next to the municipal golf course. It was, in my opinion, a rather ugly building, with its mixture of different roof heights and angles and building materials. Some parts were brick, others had wooden siding, and there was even corrugated metal in a few spots. I guess the architect thought it would look ultra-modern. I thought it looked like it was having an identity crisis.

The ducks and I made our way inside and went across the polished cement floor to the reception counter where the bright yellow box stood front and center. A flyer next to the box proclaimed that the winner of the drawing would receive a free three-day canoe rental. I smiled as I imagined paddling lazily across Paisley Lake with the ducks swimming circles around me. I filled out my card and pushed it through the slot. Upcoming activities were advertised on a bulletin board on an easel next to

CHAPTER 11

the counter. A picture of a disc-shaped object with lights evenly spaced around the perimeter caught my eye. It looked a little like Alex's spaceship. I leaned closer and read, "Come join us for Disc Golf After Dark." Frisbees in the dark? That didn't sound like any fun, especially in the rain.

The sound of heavy thumping music drew my attention to the weight room. I strolled over to the glass wall facing the foyer and looked in. The room was filled with racks of weights and machines that looked more like torture devices to me. The back wall was lined with mirrors. I watched a tall woman doing bicep curls.

She wore a green tank top and black shorts with a matching green bandana holding back her black hair. Her muscles bulged as she rhythmically alternated the weights. Lucy Cantana was a great athlete and a good bouncer. She excelled at almost every sport and had just recently won an archery competition, beating the best archer in Kirby, our rival town.

Dropping the weights, she picked up a small hand towel. Mopping the sweat from her face, she waved at me in the mirror, grabbed her water bottle, and headed for the door. The music level increased sharply as she opened it and came out to where I was. It quieted again as the door closed behind her.

"Hi, Granny," Lucy said. "What's shakin'?"

"Just dropping my name in for the contest." I nodded toward the box. "Not sure what I'll do with it if I win. I'm not much into water sports."

Lucy chuckled. "I think all of us have had enough with water for a while, although it *is* great weather for ducks." She took a big swig from her water bottle. "I guess you could give it to someone who likes fishing or something."

I snapped my fingers. "Great idea! Doc Worthington is an

avid fisherman, as is Earl Foxman, for that matter. Maybe one of them will win. As for the ducks, they are the only animals on the farm that are enjoying this weather, for sure."

Lucy frowned and said, "It's a good thing they're inside at night. There's something strange going on around here."

"What do you mean?" I thought maybe there was a pack of coyotes or foxes on the loose in the community. We had trouble with critters every once in a while, but usually, my trusty farm dogs kept them at bay. Although, they had been getting rather lazy with their night patrols.

Lucy looked around. There were folks sitting on the couches by the fireplace and an older couple walking on the indoor running track. She took a step closer to me. "Last night I had the closing shift at the restaurant and was the last one to leave. When I went out to my car, I glanced up at the sky, hoping against hope that there would be some glimmer of the moon or some stars. I'm so sick of this rain I could scream. But, instead of stars, I saw some blue and white lights sorta wobbling over the town hall across the street. It really freaked me out. I think maybe we're being watched. If I'd had my bow and arrows with me, I would've shot it out of the sky." She gave me a knowing look and took another swig of water.

I was incredulous. "You can't be serious, Lucy. You, of all people, don't really believe in UFOs and aliens and malarky like that." I laughed.

Lucy pressed her lips together and shook her head. Little drops of sweat leaped from the ends of her short, spiky hair and landed on my shirt. "I know what I saw, Granny. Either it's aliens or some secret government operation or something. I don't know, but I'm not the only one worried about it. People at the bar were talking about their own sightings last night. Some of them are ready to sell out and move away. Then there's that new cult that's moved into town."

"There you have it," I said. "You got spooked by their stories and your brain fabricated what you only *think* you saw."

"I *know* what I saw," Lucy said. "It wasn't a fabrication. You can believe me or not, but it really happened. It's not bad enough that the restaurant is losing business because people won't come out in the rain. Now we've got unidentified flying objects around town and people with green hair scaring folks. My manager told me that if things don't turn around soon, he's going to have to start laying off staff. I may be looking for another job." She turned and headed back to the weight room.

I called the ducks and headed back outside. I was a little ashamed of how dismissive I'd been, but I never expected a big, strong, self-sufficient person like Lucy Cantana to be taken in by this whole UFO scare. I wondered who the other folks were that had sighting stories. And a cult? What was becoming of my little town?

Chapter 12

I was still pondering Lucy's comments when I pulled up in front of our tiny, locally-owned grocery store, Manuel's Market. There was one of those big chain grocery stores on the other side of town near the interstate, but I preferred to support Manuel. His little shop had a great produce section in the front and a meat counter in the back where he cut his own locally-sourced beef and pork.

A young man with green hair and a nose ring was standing outside holding a stack of papers. He marched up to me and shoved one into my hand. "Be prepared," he said in a deep voice. "It's coming."

Without looking at the paper, I stuffed it in my bag and hustled inside the warm and inviting store. What made him feel it necessary to approach me so aggressively?

A little bell chimed as the ducks and I entered. I stood there for a second, trying to get my bearings back. I wasn't used to being accosted on the street. I would expect that in a big city like Las Vegas or New York, but not here in quiet, back woods Paisley Pointe.

"Buenos días, Abuela," Manuel called from where he was, down on his knees, restocking some canned goods. "Fine day to come to the store with your feathered friends. What can I be helping you with?" He was a short, stocky man with wide shoulders and an even wider smile. His kind eyes had laugh lines in the corners.

I smiled at him as I reached up to retrieve my list from its spot over my left ear. Unfolding it, I read down the page until I found the part I wanted. "Can you cut two thick pork chops and grind a pound of lean hamburger, please? And what's with the guy out front?" I couldn't help it. Alarm bells were starting to go off in my head. These strangers weren't acting like normal people.

Manuel gave me a bright smile and got up off the floor. "Sorry about that. I call the police on him, but they say sidewalk is public place. I can't do anything about it. I'll get your meat right away, Abuela." He limped to the back counter and put on his apron. When he was a young man, he had been a rodeo clown. One particularly vicious bull had tossed him into a gate, breaking his leg.

I followed him to the back where the meat cooler was, glancing over my shoulder at the man pacing back and forth in front of the store.

I stood at the counter and watched as Manuel expertly operated the big band saw and packaged the chops. As he was placing the ground beef on the scale he said, "Your ducks are so well-behaved. You don't even need to put them on a leash. My little dog, Paco, he drives me crazy. Even on a leash, he can't behave. Last night, you won't believe it." Manuel paused and wiped his hands on a towel. "I take him for his walk and he got away from me. Slipped right out of his collar. He smell a rabbit or something, I think. Took me two hours in the rain to catch him." Manuel ripped a piece of white butcher paper off the roll and arranged the hamburger in the middle. "The only reason I catch him, finally, was he got scared."

"What scared him?" I was almost afraid to ask.

Manuel's deep brown eyes got wide and he leaned forward, placing his hands on the top of the glass case. "Something came out of the sky right in front of him." He made a swooping motion with his hand.

Now I was the one leaning in. "What was it? A bird?"

Manuel straightened up and shrugged. "No sé. It not an animal. It was small and blanco with little blue lights on it. I scoop up little Paco when he turn and came back to me. We ran for home, no looking back."

The bell over the door chimed and Manuel excused himself to help another customer.

I stood there a minute, trying to think. This was getting unreal, the number of people talking about lights and things flying in the sky over Paisley Pointe. But none of them were remotely similar. Manuel's encounter sounded way different than Lucy's or Dusty's. It was probably just a kid's toy or something. Right?

A shiver went down my spine. I pulled the crumpled flier out of my market bag and read it. At the top were the now familiar purple letters. 'Perigee Prophets,' it said. 'A new world awaits us. Our new home in the heavens will be at the nearest point in its orbit on Friday. Join us Friday night in Paisley Park as we welcome the mothership and journey on to a better place.' These people couldn't really believe this, could they?

I shoved the paper back into my sack, placed my packages of meat in the shopping cart, and moved to the aisle on the farthest wall, pondering what I had learned. I knew exactly where to find everything I needed in the small store. I made my way through the aisles quickly and efficiently. The last item on my list was strawberries. I had a craving for a strawberry rhubarb pie. It had been my late husband's favorite. I had plenty of rhubarb

CHAPTER 12

in my garden at home, but this rain was not good for berries. Rounding the corner of the last shelving unit, I saw that Manuel was arguing with Wally Teller.

"Really, Mr. Teller, it is not necessary," Manuel was saying. "I do not need this *dispositititivo* ... this device." He was holding up his hands in front of him, waving them.

I rolled the cart toward the checkout and Wally spotted me. "Look!" he said, his voice rising and words coming fast. "We can test it out on Granny. I know it'll work and save you time and effort." Without waiting for Manuel's reply, Wally hopped up on the counter and began messing with the ceiling tiles. "We just attach it like so..." Wally said, "and voila! Your handy-dandy grocery helper is ready to use." He made a pose like he was one of those models who show off new products on a television game show. Then he hopped back down.

"Granny, what do you get when you cross a thought with a light bulb?" Wally was grinning from ear to ear.

"I don't know. What do you get?" I was eyeballing his contraption, not wanting to get involved, but seemingly with no choice in the matter.

"A bright idea!! Haha!"

Suspended from the ceiling was a bungee cord with a hook on the end. Wally grabbed my market bag and attached the strap to his contraption. The empty bag was hung above the counter and spun lazily. "See, no hands needed."

Manuel looked at it skeptically and began to ring up my purchases. Wally grabbed each item and eagerly stuffed it into the bag. Even Peeper and Harvey were watching the bag with rapt attention.

"Wally," I said, pointing at the bag, "isn't it getting a little too full?" The heavy bag was stretching the cord and almost touching the counter. I glanced at Manuel, who shrugged his shoulders.

"Nah," Wally said, flapping a hand, which I noticed was still bandaged from yesterday's scooter cycle spill in front of the library. "It's fine. That cord is rated for 150 pounds. Nothing to worry about."

Just then, we all heard a cracking sound and looked up. For a second, nothing happened, then a huge chunk of ceiling tile fell right on top of Wally. Harvey began quacking loudly, Peeper flapped her wings, and I started coughing from the fine white dust that floated around us.

Wally brushed bits of ceiling tile from his head. "Oops," he said, and gathering his bits and pieces, backed out the door. His face was the exact same color as the strawberries that had spilled out of the bag.

"That man is a menace," Manuel said between clenched teeth.

"He means well."

"It is not your store that he tried to ruin." Arms flailing, a rush of Spanish words flew from his mouth. I didn't need an interpreter to catch the meaning.

We managed to wipe the dust and debris from my groceries and properly replace the things that had spilled out of my bag. I offered to stay and help him clean up, but Manuel waved me off. "Not to worry, Abuela. I can do it. Have a nice day." I made up my mind to return with one of my pies to make him feel better.

I was so preoccupied with getting the dust out of my hair and off my clothing that I didn't notice Harvey was trying to tuck another treasure under his wing until we were halfway home.

"What do you have there, Harvey?" I asked. He was making little grunting sounds and using his bill to adjust his find to a more secure location. Not wanting to get stuck in the softer mud

CHAPTER 12

on the shoulder of the road, I let him keep it hidden until we pulled up to the house.

The second the golf cart stopped rolling, he attempted to make a run for it, but Peeper got in his way. I was able to grab his soft body and pull him close to me. He objected as loudly as he could while still clamping his bill around the object.

I wrestled it out of his jaws and set him down. As I inspected it, Harvey hopped around me trying to get it back. It was a very thin screwdriver with a short yellow handle. Two letters, WT, were carved into the plastic handle. I sighed, "We'll have to return this to Wally tomorrow. And you will have to apologize." I shook my finger at the beautiful mallard. He didn't look remorseful at all. He was just miffed that I wouldn't give it back.

Chapter 13

Even though I didn't take any stock in Lucy's conspiracy theories, I made extra sure that the barn doors were securely shut that night. There was something out there, that much was a fact. That many people – good, down-to-earth people – talking about seeing something in the sky, gave it credence. Then there were the greenies, as I now thought of the green-haired people popping up around town. Whether or not they were malicious remained unclear.

I lay in bed, chastising myself for not getting my name into the box for the drawing at Manuel's. In the chaos surrounding Wally's failed invention and my run-in with the 'Perigee Prophet', I had completely forgotten about it. And so, someone I didn't know ended up winning the tropical fruit basket, something I would have definitely enjoyed.

Loud braying startled me awake. I glanced at my bedside clock. It was after 11 p.m. What was wrong with Gus? I threw on jeans and a t-shirt and ran through the house. Quinn poked her head out of her room. Her hair was sticking up in all directions.

"What's going on?" she asked.

"Not sure." I stuffed my bare feet into my boots and grabbed the shotgun I kept next to the washing machine. The braying was louder and more frantic. I ran out the door. I could hear

Pearl adding her bellowing to the night. The dogs were sounding their intruder bark. Even the chickens were disturbed.

With the cloud cover, the only illumination came from the yard light installed on a tall pole near the barn. The rain appeared as diagonal lines as the drops crossed the beam from the powerful light. The light reflecting in the standing rain puddles guided my way. My heart was thumping as I trotted toward the donkey's pen on the far side of the barn. I could hear his hooves splashing as he ran circles around the corral.

"Granny, wait for me!" Quinn called. I turned and saw her flashlight bobbing in the dark. She handed me my raincoat and we rounded the corner of the barn together. I braced myself, expecting to see a pack of coyotes in mid-attack. I held the gun in front of me, ready to shoot.

Both the cow and the donkey were bucking and running around the corral. The two sheep with their lambs were cowering in a corner of their shelter.

Quinn swept her flashlight over the scene. "I don't see anything, do you?" she asked.

Climbing the fence, I said, "No, but something sure has them spooked. Did you hear any coyotes tonight?" I dropped down into the corral, leaning my gun against the rails. I attempted to snag Gus's halter as he passed me. "Try to calm Pearl down, would you? Wags! Brock! That's enough." The dogs' barking was making things worse. They came and stood next to me, growling into the darkness.

Just as I got a firm grip on Gus, something buzzed over my head. Gus let out a garbled sound and took off again, ripping my fingernail off in the process. I turned my head to track the mechanical sound, ignoring the intense pain from my finger.

"There!" I yelled, pointing. A group of flashing blue and white lights was passing over the chicken coop, heading toward the river. It sounded like a swarm of bees in flight.

Quinn swung the light up and, for just a split second, caught something shiny that looked like a plus sign in the beam. Then it was gone.

"What was that?"

I didn't answer right away, as I was attempting to calm Gus. He was foaming at the mouth and his eyes were wide and wild. I spoke softly and calmly, stroking the soft gray hair on his neck with firm pressure. After a while, he stopped sounding raspy and nuzzled the pocket where I usually kept apples and carrots.

"Sorry, old friend. I don't have any treats on me right now." I scratched his favorite spot, right between his ears, and kept one eye on the sky.

I clenched my jaw. When I caught the prankster who was scaring my animals, I was going to literally wring their neck. It was probably some teenager getting a thrill. What I had seen wasn't some alien spaceship. Someone thought they could get away with playing with people's irrational fears. Well, I wasn't going to fall into their trap.

"So, the stories around town are true," Quinn said as we made our way back to the house sometime later.

"You've been hearing about these things, too?"

Quinn nodded, snagging the tea kettle from the stove and filling it with water. "Peppermint tea?" she asked.

"You're reading my mind," I said, selecting two mugs from the cupboard. Bumping the handle of one of them brought the throbbing pain from the missing fingernail into sharp focus.

"Everyone at the city maintenance shops was comparing notes when I took my truck out to get serviced today." She plucked two teabags from a box and put them in the mugs. "The strange thing is, depending on when and where they saw it, everyone's description was different. Almost like there's more than one of those things out there."

"I thought that, too," I said. We talked over our tea for a while, allowing the warm beverage to work its magic on our frayed nerves.

Chapter 14

I didn't think I would sleep well, but the next thing I knew, my alarm was forcing me out of bed. Snooze buttons don't work well on farms. Animals depended on us to take care of their needs. They didn't care that you had been up late the night before chasing UFOs.

"Good morning, Paisley Pointe. This is Wally Teller, your weather feller, with your daily weather report. We are on day eight now of this low-pressure system. It seems to have stalled out right over us like an old car with a bad starter. Sorry to disappoint you, folks. What might cheer you up, though, is that we aren't the only ones getting waterlogged. The whole valley is under this system. Upstream from us in Kirby, they are reporting record amounts of rainfall as well."

I groggily flipped the bacon in the frying pan and thought about the man from Kirby that I'd met during the archery competition, Teddy Schneider. I wondered how he was holding up in this depressing weather. Too bad I didn't get his number. He had been quite the gentleman. I could have invited him to the dance.

"Don't forget to enter your name in today's drawings being held at Divina's Blooms and the Harp Street Vet Clinic. Some amazing prizes, folks. Support our local businesses and maybe win some swag in the process. Hey did you hear about the outlet that got in a fight with the extension cord? He thought he could socket to him! Ha ha! This is Wally Teller, your weather feller, signing off."

"Has it really only been eight days?" Quinn asked, sitting at the table. "It feels like at least a month." She buttered a piece of toast and dunked it in her egg yolk. "If the sun doesn't come out soon, I think I'm going to go crazy!"

The dogs jumped up from their bed in the laundry room and began barking. It was their 'we've got company' bark. They ran outside through their doggy door and Quinn and I looked out the window. A large black van was coming into the farm yard with its two-dog escort. A young man wearing a black suit cautiously stepped out and opened an umbrella.

I unlatched the screen door and called the dogs. They reluctantly left their sniffing posts and returned to their bed. "Hello!" I called. "What can I help you with?"

The young bearded man made his way to the sidewalk and approached the steps. He looked up at me and asked, "Is there a Quinn Nicholson here?"

"Come on in," I said. I noticed a name tag just below his red pocket square. "Brendan, is it? I'm Irma Appleton. Quinn is in the kitchen."

Brendan politely wiped his shoes and shook the water from his umbrella as he stepped into the laundry room. He followed me into the kitchen and took the proffered chair across from Quinn.

"Can I offer you some coffee this morning?" I asked.

Shaking his head, Brendan said, "No thank you, ma'am. I appreciate the offer, though." He looked at Quinn and asked, "Are you Quinn Nicholson?"

When she nodded, he said, "I was sent by LuxArt Galleries. May I please see some identification to ensure that I am speaking with the right person?" He ducked his head apologetically. He was trying his best to sound serious, but his voice cracked about every third word.

After examining Quinn's driver's license and handing it back, Brendan reached into the inside pocket of his jacket and extracted two envelopes. I sat next to Quinn, curious. I knew this was none of my business and that I should leave the room. But I couldn't tear myself away.

He opened the first envelope and unfolded a single sheet of paper. "Sign here, please, to indicate receipt of documents." He pulled a pen out of his shirt pocket and used it to indicate the line he was referring to.

Securing the paper back inside its envelope, he offered Quinn the second envelope and stood up. "Have a nice day, ladies." He gave a little bow and headed back out in the rain.

Quinn stared at the envelope in her hand and then looked at me.

"Well, open it!" The suspense was killing me.

Quinn flipped it over and broke the fancy wax seal embossed with a loopy capital L. She pulled out some papers and unfolded them. Clipped to the top page was a check for $25,000. My eyes bugged out at the amount. Her mouth dropped open. I gripped Quinn's arm and stared at the number. "Is this for real?" I whispered.

She pulled the check from under the paperclip and held it up to the light. A watermark could clearly be seen. "Looks real to me!" She looked at me and paused. Then, squealing, we hugged each other.

"How... What... Who?" I couldn't form a complete sentence to

CHAPTER 14

save my life.

Laughing, Quinn said, "This is quite the mystery, isn't it? I'm not sure what's going on, either." She turned to the pages laying on the table. "This is a contract! LuxArt wants to show more of my work." She scanned the pages quickly. "They're sending an agent out on Saturday to look at my art." She dropped the papers onto the table and leaned back, covering her face and groaning. "What am I going to do?"

"What do you mean?" Her reaction wasn't what I was expecting. Before her falling out with Ricardo, Quinn had been excited to be the next up-and-coming artist and break onto the New York art scene. Now here she was, acting like she was going to the dentist for a root canal. "Isn't this what you had always dreamed of? This is your big opportunity."

"It is," Quinn said, sitting up and fiddling with the envelope. "I just... it's just..." She took a deep breath. "After what happened last year, I never thought I'd have another shot at my dream." She turned toward me with the saddest look I'd ever seen. "It broke me inside, you know? I didn't think I was good enough. Now, to see that maybe I am, it's a shock." She gave me a wobbly smile and squeezed my hand. "I'd better get to work. We can talk more about this later."

She disappeared into her room, leaving the papers in the middle of the table. Returning a few minutes later, she kissed the top of my head and said, "If you are going to visit the vet clinic this morning, could you pick up some udder cream? I used the last of it this morning." There was a lightness in her step as I watched her leave.

Chapter 15

I puttered around the house for a while, picking up and putting things away. Dusting the living room, I paused in front of a painting that Quinn had given me for my 65th birthday. It was a watercolor depicting an aspen grove. Sunlight was streaming through the leaves into a small glade, where a deer and its fawn were grazing. There was a sense of peace and tranquility that calmed me every time I looked at it. I could almost hear the rustle of the leaves and smell the fresh air. Quinn had captured the essence of the aspen grove.

I was having such a hard time getting motivated to do anything. Maybe it was the lack of sleep or the excitement of our late-night adventure. I don't know, but I felt like my head was full of cobwebs.

I returned to the kitchen and poured myself another cup of coffee. Maybe the caffeine would clear my brain and get me moving. As I sat there, my mind returned to last night's scare. How frightened the animals had been, how long it had taken to calm them down. Pearl's milk production this morning was about half of what it normally was. The more I thought about it, the angrier I became. I still didn't think it was an extraterrestrial scoping out my barnyard. Whoever was behind this was going to get a piece of my mind. I thought about all the stories I'd heard this week from my neighbors and friends, and how I hadn't believed them. Now armed with first-hand knowledge, I felt at once ashamed and fired up.

Slapping my hands down on the tabletop, I stood to my feet and reached for my rain gear. It was time to bring out the big guns. The throbbing in my finger only fueled my anger more.

Quacking sounds greeted me as I stepped onto the back porch. How anyone could be happy in such dismal weather was beyond me, but both ducks had perma-grins on their faces as I let them into the golf cart. I placed my heavy market bag gently onto the back seat. A little sweet persuasion can go a long way and I knew just how to serve it up.

Driving up Main Street to the rhythm of the bricks under my tires, I noticed how bedraggled the flower boxes in front of the businesses were becoming. This spring, Quinn had filled them with beautiful annuals like petunias and marigolds. She interspersed the flowers with trailing ivy and other greens. Everything was so waterlogged that the plants looked like drunken sailors on shore leave. When would this rain end? Our little town was beginning to come apart at the seams.

Flipping a U-turn on the street, I pulled up in front of Divina's Blooms facing her big display window and parked between two of the so-called prophets' vehicles. A group of them stood huddled together under her awning, holding placards. One said, 'The end is coming!' Another one read, 'It's not too late. Join us.' The last one I read had a picture of a spaceship and the words 'Mothership, we are ready!' The 'prophets' didn't look too happy to be standing there. Most of them looked like they could use a sandwich.

I grumbled to myself and looked past them to the large plate-glass window of the shop. Today it held an old bicycle, the kind with the luggage rack in the back and metal basket attached to the handlebars. The basket overflowed with daisies and gladiolus blooms, a garland of greenery wound through the frame, and on the back was an old-fashioned picnic basket full of roses. It was bright and cheerful, just like the shop's owner. With the steady beat of rain on the roof of the cart, I sat for a moment to admire my good friend's artistic display. She always came up with the most creative ways to show off her flowers.

The old wooden floors creaked as I stepped inside. Sniffing appreciatively at the mix of eucalyptus, lavender, and roses, I glanced around. Antique furniture was arranged around the space with knickknacks, containers, and gifts placed just so. A marble-topped sideboard served as the sales desk off to one side.

Divina squealed when she saw me and came from behind her workstation with her arms open wide. "Granny! It's so good to see you!" When she finally pulled back, I discreetly brushed a few cat hairs off my shirt before answering. Divina's two Persian cats had free reign of the shop. I had made sure Harvey and Peeper were sleeping snugly in the golf cart before I entered the store. I didn't know how the cats would react to my gregarious companions and didn't feel that today was the day to make introductions.

"It's good to see you, too, Divina. How are you?" I held her at arm's length and took in her long, curly gray hair and turquoise peasant blouse. She reminded me of a gypsy.

Divina parted her bright red lips and gave me a toothy smile. She used one hand to smooth her freshly dyed blonde hair behind her ear. I noticed a slight tremble. "Oh, you know. Hanging in there." She took my hand and led me to a dining table covered with baby shower trinkets. "Let's get comfortable, shall we?"

CHAPTER 15

We sat down and she picked up a small glass figurine, turning it over and over. Glancing toward the back of the store where the cold room was, she leaned forward. Lowering her voice, she said, "Truth is, Granny, I'm worried. These new people here in town," she glanced out the window at the demonstrators. "They seem to know what they are talking about. What if it's real? Are they coming here to harm us? Or are they going to take us to a higher plane?" Her eyes grew big. "What if they are going to harvest our organs?"

I reached out and took the fragile glass bear from her hands and set it on the other side of the table. As shaky as she was, I was afraid she would drop it. I covered her hands with my own. "Divina, there's nothing to worry about. I'm sure there's a logical explanation for what's going on. There is no alien spaceship."

I looked down as I felt something brush against my leg. It was the gray cat.

Divina shot another look toward the back. "Sterling and I heard noises last night. There was a banging sound. At first, we thought that Princess and Clementine were trying to get into the cabinets. They do that sometimes. But then we realized that it was coming from the living room window. Sterling got up to see what it was. When he got to the front of the house, there was some disc-shaped thing hovering over the trees across the street. You know those people are camping there, right?" She pointed a bejeweled finger toward the park.

I knew that Divina and Sterling lived in the apartment over their store. How could something be hitting the second-story window in the middle of the night? I followed her finger and tried to imagine what they had seen. I wondered what color the disc had been.

"He doesn't act like it now, but I know it totally freaked him out. Me, too. The cats were on edge and refused to settle down. We sat up the rest of the night on the couch, watching to see if it was going to come back."

Just then the floor gave a loud creak. Divina jumped and covered her face. A tiny squeak, like a mouse, came out.

Mayor Sterling Springer closed the door to the back room and walked over to us, adjusting his two-toned blue tie. There were dark circles under his eyes, but he was freshly showered and shaved.

"Good morning, ladies," he said, a smidgen too brightly. "I'm running a bit behind this morning, but couldn't leave for work without kissing my beautiful bride."

Divina stood up and hugged her husband. As they pulled apart, I saw a look pass between them, and Sterling gave a slight shake of his head. Divina lowered her head and straightened his already perfect tie.

In his best campaign voice, he said, "Have a wonderful day, Granny. See you tonight, dear." He returned the way he'd come after shooting daggers with his eyes out the front window and shut the door softly behind him.

"Oh, Granny. Don't tell anyone what I said. Sterling doesn't want people to know. He's afraid that they will think he's crazy. And with his re-election just a few months away, he doesn't want to risk any negative publicity." She was flailing her arms and looked like she was about to cry.

He should be trying to get to the bottom of this instead of worrying about his image, I thought. I cast a look around the shop for a way to distract her and saw the big yellow box near her cash register. "I nearly forgot! I want to put my name in the drawing. What are you giving away, Divina?"

CHAPTER 15

Like I'd flipped a switch, Divina's expression changed. Her eyes sparkled as she rushed across the room to get me an entry card and pen. "I've come up with a *gorgeous* arrangement. Sunflowers, of course." She emphasized the *sun* with a little head tilt.

Sitting right next to the box was a large galvanized tin watering can. Spilling out of the top were bright yellow sunflowers. Curly ferns peeked out between the cheerful petals as did bright blue delphiniums. It was stunning.

Fingering one of the ferns, I said, "Oh, Divina, this is lovely. You brought back some sunshine."

She beamed and clasped her hands under her chin. Her long prairie skirt swished from side to side. "Thank you. It does lift the spirits, doesn't it?" For a moment, she looked like her usual happy self, then her shoulders sagged once more.

I filled out my card and dropped it in the box. Then I had Divina help me pick out a hanging basket filled with pink and purple petunias for my niece, Vivian's, birthday. After arranging for the delivery, I hugged Divina and made my way to the door.

"Remember, mum's the word on that whole UFO thing," Divina said. She put a long, graceful finger to her lips. "Sterling would be very upset if he knew I told you about that."

"I won't say a word," I promised, clasping her shoulders gently, "but I will try to get to the bottom of it. The whole town is in a tizzy over it."

Back in the golf cart, I retrieved my list from under my wig and crossed off the first of my errands. Sighing resolutely, I tucked it back in and patted my red hair.

Reversing out of my parking spot, I glanced up and noticed that Divina was still at the front window. I waved at her and set off. Thankfully the demonstrators had moved off down the street.

Our town hall is set back from a side street just a block past Main, right across from the Pointe of No Return, a favorite local pub. The ducks and I waddled into the lobby and made our way across the tile floor to the front desk of our police department. It occupied the space right next to the county clerk's office. Further down was the mayor's office. I glanced over to make sure Sterling wasn't around. It might make him suspicious to see me here after coming to the flower shop.

The young officer behind the window was busily typing on the computer and didn't look up when I approached. He had short, ink-black hair and deep brown skin. His uniform was slightly rumpled but clean. I recognized him as being one of Lucy Cantana's workout buddies from the gym. I tapped on the bullet-proof glass to get his attention. He jumped back like he'd been snake bitten, the chair shooting backward. His face reddened as he rolled his chair back to the desk.

"I'm so sorry about that, Javier," I giggled. "You must have been concentrating super hard. I thought all officers had some kind of spidey sense so people can't sneak up on them."

With a shy grin, he said, "Normally you're right, Granny. I guess I'm just really tired today. I was trying to finish this report so I can go home."

"Were you working last night, too?" I asked.

He nodded. "Usually not a big deal, but I spent a good chunk of my shift taking calls about these crazy alien folks and trying to chase down these strange blue lights I saw. We got tons of calls about them and the chief has us all on high alert. I didn't believe all the hype until I actually saw them for myself. I watched it get hit by a bolt of lightning and fall from the sky, too. It was awesome. But I never was able to find it." He pinched the bridge of his nose and blinked.

"Speaking of the chief," I said, "is he in? I brought him something." I held up my market bag.

Javier pushed a button and the door next to him buzzed and unlocked. When Harvey came through the door and saw Javier, he quacked in greeting. Grinning, Javier said, "What's up, duck?" and reached out a hand to stroke Harvey's beautiful green head. "You know you work in a small town when ducks walk into the police department for a visit."

I led the way down the hall and knocked on Chief Ellis's door. Buck was family, having married Vivian, my niece. I was proud of the work he was doing in our community but felt that maybe a little persuasion was in order to settle this UFO situation once and for all.

The chief's office was what I would call professionally masculine. The chairs were covered in hunter-green leather. An American flag stood proudly behind the desk on one side, while a red Marine Corps flag graced the other. The large solid desk was made of dark wood and looked as immovable as I knew the chief could be. But I had a secret weapon.

Buck stood up and came around the desk. "Granny! I'm so glad to see you!" He enveloped my small frame in a bear hug and just about squeezed the stuffing out of me. I looked up at him and noticed the five o'clock shadow and the deep lines on his forehead. He greeted the ducks in turn, too. "Good of you to drop by, Peeper. Nice to see you again, Harvey." Peeper settled under one of the chairs while Harvey made a lap of the room, looking for stray office supplies.

"Good to see you, too, Buck. You look beat, though. Tough day?" I glanced at the clock on the wall. "A little early to be looking so haggard."

He ran a hand through his salt and pepper hair and nodded. "I'm sure you've heard about all the unidentified flying objects that have invaded our town as well as our, um, visitors. I can't seem to track down the source of the UFOs. There's nothing consistent in the sightings, other than their showing up around the same time as these people."

I placed my market bag on the desk and reached inside. "Maybe this will cheer you up."

Buck grinned and rubbed his hands together. "Peach pie? My favorite! Let me go and get some plates and forks."

I reached into the bag again, "I've got that covered, Buck. Have a seat and let me serve you."

"Always prepared, aren't you?" Buck laughed and went back around his desk. Soon we were enjoying the sweet taste of cinnamon and peaches.

"Granny, you spoil me," Buck said, wiping his lips with a napkin. "Don't tell Vivian that I like your pies best." He winked at me and helped himself to another slice.

Wrapping the tin foil around the remaining pie, I said, "Please take the rest home and share it with her." I paused, wiping some crumbs off the highly polished desk. "Buck, I don't think you're doing enough with these alien seekers. Or the UFO sightings." I looked him in the eye.

"Aaaannnnddd there it is," Buck said, his voice going deeper. "I was waiting for the other shoe to drop." His face flushed and the lines on his forehead became even deeper. "We're doing everything we can, Granny, trust me." He started ticking off his fingers, "I've doubled my nightly patrols. All the officers are working overtime. I've added another dispatcher to handle the incoming calls. We're following up on leads as fast as we can. I can't devote ALL my resources to this silly problem. There are

CHAPTER 15

other issues to take care of, too, you know. Those people, as annoying as they are, have constitutional rights. They haven't broken any laws." He ran a hand through his thick hair.

I sat primly on the edge of my seat. "Are you about finished with your temper tantrum?" I asked, crossing my arms and tilting my head. "I didn't come here to berate you. I came here to offer a suggestion. And this isn't some silly problem. The citizens in this community are scared, Buck. I have it on good authority that some are even thinking of leaving over all this."

Buck's shoulders slumped and he had the good sense to look contrite. "I'm sorry. I should have known that you wouldn't be like all the armchair quarterbacks we have around here, sitting in coffee shops, solving the world's problems. Everyone seems to think that they can do this job better than we can." He leaned back in his chair and tented his fingers. "So, what is your brilliant idea?" He took a deep breath and waited.

I took my time, sitting back and smoothing the fabric on my shirt. I patted my hair and crossed my legs. After pinching the crease in my pants, I said, "Steal their thunder." I waited to see if the weather would back me up. No rumbles came from the sky.

Buck opened his mouth to speak and I held up my hand. "Just hear me out." I watched Buck as he forced himself to relax in his chair.

I reached back into my bag and pulled out the flier I'd been forced to take outside of Manuel's Market. I slid it across the desk. "Hold a Town Hall meeting at the same time that these 'Perigee Prophets' are holding their party on Friday night. Draw away their crowd." I tapped the paper. "Give the townsfolk something else to focus on." I shifted in my seat, careful not to kick the duck I knew was under there. "You also need more eyes on the sky. I've seen one of those things myself. It scared the living daylights out of my livestock last night. Whatever they are, they're quick, and because they are airborne, they don't have to follow roads. I'm more than convinced that these so-called prophets are behind them, using scare tactics to convince people to donate money or join their cause."

Buck shifted in his seat and picked up a letter opener to fiddle with. His eyes drifted to the pictures of his family on the wall. A rumble of thunder sounded outside, rattling the window behind him.

I cleared my throat and waited for his full attention. "Call a town meeting, Buck. Get everyone together and enlist their help. Give them something positive to do so they don't just sit around speculating and worrying. Create a nightly schedule and have people sign up for shifts. The more people we have looking for these things, the more likely we are to trap one or find out the mastermind behind this cockamamie scare."

Buck leaned forward and put his elbows on the desk. He nodded thoughtfully. "Yeah! A citizen's patrol. We could divide the town into sectors and if someone sees one of the UFOs, we could coordinate its movements and track it." He pulled a pad of paper out of a drawer and started scribbling. "We could track these cult people, too, without appearing to do so. Keep them on the up-and-up."

"I'm sure the radio station would advertise your meeting as a Public Service Announcement," I said, standing up. I gathered my bag and called the ducks.

Buck stood and came around the desk. He enveloped me in another bear hug, which was quite uncomfortable, what with his bulletproof vest and all. "Thanks, Granny. For the pie, as well as the talk." He walked me and the ducks to the lobby.

CHAPTER 15

Officer Ramos waved as we left. "Great weather for ducks!" he grinned.

I smiled at him and nodded as I held the door open. That line was sure getting a workout this week.

"And that's how you get things done," I said to the ducks as we left the parking lot. Peeper half-closed her eyes and peeped at me. Harvey just ignored me and tucked the paperclip he'd scored under his wing.

Chapter 16

The Harp Street Veterinary Clinic was located in a modern-style brick building just behind Main Street. Living on a farm, you get used to the more, shall we say, earthy smells that come with dealing with animals. But when you add that semi-sweet antiseptic cleaner smell to it, something changes. I wrinkled my nose as I approached the front desk.

Eryn McLoughlin, the young, attractive receptionist, was sitting at the computer. Normally she was dressed in a t-shirt and shorts and a ponytail. Today, she wore her hair in long curls that reached past her shoulders and eyeliner that ended in wings. The fake eyelashes she was wearing looked a little like caterpillars sitting on her eyelids. Her polo shirt barely contained her ample chest with the top buttons undone to show her cleavage. She looked up and smiled when she saw me.

"Hello, Granny." She glanced at the calendar on her desk and frowned. "I don't have you scheduled for an appointment today. Is everything OK?"

"Everything's fine," I said. The ducks said the same.

She stood up and leaned over the counter. I caught a whiff of some expensive-smelling perfume. "And it's good to see you, too," she said to the ducks. Looking back at me she said, "This is great weather for ducks, am I right?"

CHAPTER 16

I bit my tongue to keep from making a snarky comment. Instead, I turned to the bright yellow box sitting on the counter and picked up a pen. "I just came by to sign up for the giveaway. I'd love to say hi to Doc if he's here." I scribbled my information and dropped the card inside. The clinic was giving away three days of free pet boarding. I couldn't imagine that they would want to board all my animals. I guess I could always give it away to one of my town friends if I won.

The door leading to the back rooms opened and an unfamiliar man in a spotless white lab coat came out. He had a bright yellow Frisbee in his hand that he kept twirling. He was young and had sandy hair and green eyes. The ducks went over to check him out. "Hey, what's this?" he asked, laughing. He knelt down and ran his large hand down Peeper's back.

Eryn giggled and said, "Steve, meet Harvey and Peeper. Harvey, Peeper, this is Steve." She batted her long eyelashes.

I cleared my throat. "Hello. I'm Irma. Irma Appleton. Everyone calls me Granny."

Steve straightened up and said, "Oh, hi! I didn't see you there. I'm Steve Mitchell. I'm the new lab tech." He crossed the floor and shook my hand. "That's a handsome pair of ducks you have there. Did you know that mallards don't dive? They are known as dabble eaters, picking up insect larvae and aquatic vegetation around the edges of ponds. What happened to the mallard's wing, if you don't mind my asking?" He pointed to Harvey's droopy side. I had grown so used to seeing his lopsided gait that I didn't pay attention to it anymore.

"He was shot with an arrow in the park where you play your disc golf," Eryn interjected. "Isn't that terrible?" She sidled up next to Steve and put a hand on his sleeve. I think she could have climbed into his pocket if she stood any closer. "He'll never be able to fly again." Her sigh was so big that I felt the air move.

"Are you here to have it looked at?" Steve asked, completely ignoring Eryn, kneeling again and gently probing Harvey's wing.

I shook my head. "No, he's fine. All healed up now. Doc Worthington did a great job of patching him. What I do need is some udder cream. Do you think you could fetch some for me?"

Steve nodded enthusiastically and excused himself.

Eryn walked back to her computer and sat down. Her shoulders were slumped and her lips were drawn up in a pout. It all made sense now.

I went around the desk and stood next to her. I whispered, "You need to just be yourself. Quit trying so hard. If it's meant to be, it will happen." I patted her arm and smiled gently. I'd known Eryn since she was a toddler. She was like another granddaughter to me.

Eryn looked at me and her eyes filled with tears. She reached out and hugged me.

Steve burst through the connecting door holding a box over his head. "I found it!" he exclaimed.

Eryn swiveled her chair quickly and reached for a tissue. I moved to the end of the counter away from her and took the box from him. Glancing at the poor girl from the corner of my eye, I asked, "Is this the only kind you carry? I don't recognize this packaging. How much should I use?"

I only half-listened to his response. I was more interested in watching Eryn dab at her eyes and button up her shirt. Atta girl. Smiling to myself, I tucked the box into my pocket and turned to go.

Back at the farm, I made lunch for Quinn and myself. These daily trips to town were taking up more of my time than I had realized. Not that I could do much around the farm with all the

CHAPTER 16

rain, but still, there were things that needed to be taken care of. Even with Quinn's help, the list of chores was lengthy.

Not long after Quinn returned to work, I was up to my elbows in pie dough. The churches in Paisley Pointe took turns hosting a weekly community dinner. It was our turn this Sunday and of course, I had volunteered to bake pies. I had a freezer full of baking apples from my orchard already diced up and ready to go, so I grabbed enough to make a dozen pies. The radio was on and I was singing along at the top of my lungs. Just as I pulled the first batch out of the oven, the phone rang.

"Good afternoon, Granny," came the deep baritone voice of Doc Worthington. "I'm so glad I caught you!"

Doc and I have been friends for a long time. He is the only vet in town and cared not only for all the cats and dogs and other assorted pets but also made regular rounds to the farms in the area. I could count on him stopping by to see my animals at least once a week. I'm not sure he visited all the farms that often, but I have a hunch it probably had something to do with his penchant for sweets.

I've never met a man who has a more tender heart toward animals than Doc. He once stayed up all night with one of my ewes when she was having trouble lambing triplets. He refused to put down stray animals, too. He kept them in kennels at the clinic and found homes for them, frequently taking them to his own home to foster them.

"I've got an unusual request," he said. I pictured him pulling at his hair as he talked. It always seemed to be standing on end, like a mad scientist's doo.

I had heard this before. Many of the animals on my farm had come from his 'unusual requests'. Gus the mule was a great example. Doc had asked me if I would take Gus after his owner had passed away. I'm a softie and Doc knows it. I would never turn away an animal in need. "Shoot," I said. "Whatcha got for me today? A litter of kittens? Another goose?"

"A llama."

"Come again?"

"A llama."

"Where'd you get a llama?" I asked, my eyes wide. I didn't know the first thing about caring for a llama.

I could hear talking in the background. "I just found him. I'm out on my rounds. He was stuck in the mud at the edge of the river. It took some doing to get him out. He's pretty weak. Don't know how long he'd been there. Will you take him? Just until we find his owners?"

I didn't even take a second to think. "Of course, I will. Do you need me to come and get him?" I clicked into rescue mode, thinking of all I needed to do to get ready for this llama.

"No, I've got help. I was out at the Dodson place with a lame horse. Chris brought his horse trailer down and helped me get this guy out of the mud. His farm is on the verge of getting flooded out, so I don't want to leave the llama there. Chris has enough to worry about right now."

"Bring him to the barn. I'll go out and get one of the stalls ready for him right now." I hung up the phone and headed outside. Taking bales of straw I made a deep bed in the first stall for the new guest. I filled the water tank and put hay in the rack. By the time I was finished, I could hear a diesel truck backing toward the barn.

Doc Worthington hopped out of his big truck and guided Chris to get the trailer as close to the barn doors as possible. The barn cats rubbed against my legs as we watched. When the truck stopped, I stepped out into the rain, opened the trailer gate, and

CHAPTER 16

got my first glimpse of a mud-covered, waterlogged, bedraggled animal.

The llama was lying down with his head stretched out on the floorboards. Even to my untrained eye, it was easy to see that this poor guy was in bad shape. I moved out of the way as Doc and Chris worked to get him to stand. They rolled him onto his sternum, but the second they let go, the llama slumped back to his side.

I ran back into the barn and returned with a large burlap sack. "Here, get this around his middle like a sling. Then we can lift him up and help him walk." I placed the bag next to the llama and tucked it under its belly as far as I could. The men pushed him over and Doc grabbed the end of the sack. Chris came to my side and we managed to get the animal in a standing position. Half dragging and half stumbling, we got him into the barn and onto the straw in his box.

A clap of thunder rumbled outside. "You folks mind if I head for home?" Chris asked. "I hate to be away too long. We've been watching the river rise steadily and may need to evacuate soon."

Doc shook Chris's hand. "Thanks for the help, Dodson. I couldn't have done this without you."

"Let me know if you need me to house any of your animals," I added. "Or if you, Laurie, and the kids need a place to stay. I've got an air mattress and plenty of blankets."

Chris shook my hand and said, "We may just take you up on that offer, Granny. Talk to you soon." He ran back out into the rain and left.

While Doc hurried back out to his truck for medical equipment, I used the burlap to rub down the shivering llama. He was covered in so much mud and muck that I couldn't make out what color he was. It was alarming how limp the poor guy was.

Doc returned with a clear bag filled with liquid and we hung it from a wire attached to the sideboards. He inserted a needle into the llama's neck and we watched with bated breath. After what seemed like an eternity, the llama sighed and opened his eyes.

"Let's push him up onto his chest," Doc said. "He's still not out of the woods." He pulled on his hair and made it stand on end. If I wasn't wearing a wig, I would have done the same. Instead, I silently prayed for the llama to recover. We pushed on his shoulder and rolled him upright. This time, he stayed that way and tucked his front legs under his chest. He raised his head up and looked soulfully at Doc with his big dark eyes. I would kill for lashes that long.

A few minutes later, he struggled to his feet, swaying a little bit. So, we put our makeshift strap back under his belly and stood on either side of him. His ears perked up and he started sniffing around. He zeroed in on the hay rack and stumbled toward it. Pulling tufts of hay out, he began to chew.

"That's the ticket!" Doc exclaimed. He looked like a father whose child just received a gold medal. He rubbed his hand along the llama's back. We continued to watch our patient, who was looking better by the minute. The IV bag was getting close to empty and he'd made a dent in the hay supply. It was nice and cozy in the loose box, with the sound of rain drumming on the roof.

"I think I'll name him Mark Spitz, after the Olympic swimmer," I said. "We'll call him Spitz for short."

Doc tilted his head and pushed his glasses up on his nose. He chuckled. "Oh, the irony! Spitz, you are one lucky llama, even if you can't swim."

Spitz turned his head and looked at Doc, chewing non-stop.

CHAPTER 16

He blinked his long eyelashes and touched his nose to Doc's forehead.

I laughed. "I think that was llama talk for 'thank you'!"

Doc rubbed the wet spot and grinned. "First time I've been kissed by a llama, that's for sure." He removed the needle and unhooked the deflated IV bag from the wall. "I think Spitz is well on the way to recovering. It's beyond me how he ended up in the mud. My guess is that he fell in the river somewhere upstream – maybe he was trying to cross it – and the current was so strong it carried him away."

I shuddered to think of all that Spitz had gone through. From falling into the water, being swept downstream, desperately trying to get to shore, and finally getting stuck in the mud and struggling to free himself. Rubbing the side of Spitz's neck, I said, "You're safe now, buddy."

"Hello?" came a voice from outside. "Granny? Are you in here? I saw Doc's truck outside. Is everything OK?"

Startled, I glanced at my watch. "In here, Quinn," I called. "Goodness, look at the time! I didn't realize it was getting so late."

Quinn peeked over the door. "Who's this?" she asked. "Hey, Doc."

Doc raised a hand in greeting and said, "Hi there, Quinn. Meet Spitz, the worst swimmer in the llama Olympics. He's going to be staying here for a while."

"He's so cute!" Quinn lifted the latch and came inside. Spitz took a step toward her and put his head on her shoulder. "Aww, he likes me." She petted the top of his head. "Where'd he come from?"

"We don't know. Possibly up by Kirby someplace. Looks like he's going to be fine, now that he's more hydrated and out of the cold and wet."

"Speaking of cold and wet, how about we go on up to the house and have something to warm us up?" I asked. "I'm thinking grilled cheese sandwiches and soup. What do you say, Doc? Want to stay for dinner?"

Doc gave a weary smile. "That's music to my ears. I could use some sustenance after all that. I haven't eaten since breakfast."

When we walked into the house, I realized two things. One, I'd left the radio playing, and two, the oven was still on. Luckily, I hadn't had any pies baking, or we would probably have had the fire department visiting as well.

Groaning, Doc dropped his tall frame onto one of the kitchen chairs. I turned off the oven and pulled a pan out of the cabinet. Quinn went and changed out of her work clothes. "How does chicken noodle sound?" I asked.

"I don't know. How does it sound?" Doc had a sly grin on his tired face. "I imagine it clucks."

"Very funny. I meant would you like to eat some chicken noodle soup? I also have tomato if you'd rather have that." I rolled my eyes at him.

"Tomato goes great with grilled cheese. Thank you for having me. And thank you for helping me with Spitz." Doc got up and went to the cupboard. He started setting the table. I like a man who knows his way around a kitchen, even if he does have the corniest jokes ever.

I went to the freezer in the laundry room and came back with a bag of soup. Nothing in this house came from a can. Not when I could make it myself, and I haven't had any complaints yet.

"What's this?" Doc asked, holding up the contract from LuxArt.

Quinn grabbed it and folded it back up. "It's nothing," she

CHAPTER 16

said, ducking her head.

"Now, Quinn," I chastised, "it's not nothing." I waved the spatula I was holding. "Quinn got a contract from an art gallery. They want to show her work. Isn't that fabulous?"

"Congratulations!" Doc grabbed Quinn and hugged her. "I'm so proud of you."

"Thanks," she said, flushing. "I'm not sure if I'm going to go through with it."

A clash of cymbals from the radio made all of us jump. "And now, a public service announcement. A Town Hall Meeting is being held in the high school gym on Friday night at 7 p.m. That's tomorrow folks. Police Chief Buck Ellis requests your presence to discuss the unusual sightings that have been happening all around town. He has a plan, folks, and needs your help. Attend the meeting and be part of getting to the bottom of this problem.

"This is Wally Teller, your weather feller. The rain is going to continue, folks, right on through the weekend. Water levels are rising, so be careful out there. Never drive through standing water. You never know just how deep it is or how fast it might be flowing. Don't be a silly willy."

The opening chords to "Walking on Sunshine" began playing. I brought the soup and sandwiches to the table and we all took our seats. "And now our nightly giveaway winners! The lovely sunflower bouquet from Divina's Blooms is going to Mandy Kendall. Hey, Mandy, what do you call a beehive without an exit? Un-bee-leave-able! Haha! And the winner of the three nights of pet boarding, courtesy of the Harp Street Vet Clinic is Harlan Oakes. Harlan, do you know how to keep a bull from charging? Take away its credit card! Haha! Remember, folks, your entries are going into the big drawing for the weekend getaway, so don't lose hope. Come to the dance on Saturday night to find out if you are the winner. That's all for now. This is Wally Teller, your weather feller, signing off."

As the music resumed, Doc smiled, "That Wally. He's something else." He chuckled. "Did he ever show you his solution to keep squirrels from stealing birdseed?"

Quinn and I looked at each other and shook our heads. "No. I've seen some of his other 'inventions'," I said, using air quotes, "but not that one."

"Well, let me tell you about this high-tech piece of work," Doc said, leaning back and stretching out his long legs. "First, he found some kind of spring. It looked like one of those kid's toys that you can walk down a flight of stairs. He attached it to the underside of his bird feeder." Doc started chuckling.

"I've seen those before," I said. "Wally didn't invent those."

Doc held up a finger. "Wait. There's more. He decided to *improve* on that invention. Do you know how?" He started laughing so hard he couldn't finish for a minute. "He rigged it to one of those air horns and every time a squirrel stretched the spring, that air horn would go off!" Doc held his stomach and guffawed.

I couldn't help myself. I started laughing, too. Quinn joined in and the three of us laughed so hard we cried. The mental image of that poor startled squirrel running for cover when the horn sounded sent me into another fit.

As Doc wiped his eyes with the back of his hand, he said, "The best part was, he tried it out in his front yard. A squirrel set it off just as Beverly Baker was walking by with her prissy little Pomeranian! She called the cops on him and chased Wally for two blocks with her cane."

Beverly Baker had a reputation in town for being the biggest bully around. She was always on the lookout for anyone who was even the slightest bit out of line. People had been known to cross the street to avoid her. She was a vigilante on a crusade to rid Paisley Pointe of law-breakers.

I burst out in another fit of giggles. "Poor Wally. None of his inventions ever work, but they're harmless. I can just picture her swatting at him with her cane. Lucky for him, he can run faster than she can." My sides hurt from laughing so hard.

Chapter 17

Tucking my errand list into my short red spiky wig Friday morning, I headed out the door. I checked on Spitz one last time. He was standing in his stall with his head over the door, eyes wide and fearful. His breathing was labored and shallow. He emitted a high-pitched whining noise every time I took a step in his direction. I wanted to give him a bath but knew I needed to hold off until he was completely comfortable with me.

Harvey and Peeper were ready and waiting by the golf cart when I made my way across the lake that used to be my farmyard. I squished toward them, glaring at the sky. This weather was enough to make anyone grumpy. Over breakfast, Wally had announced that the storm should pass by Monday, but that seemed ages away.

On the bright side, one of the day's giveaways was at Something Nice, my friend Nora's bakery. I was looking forward to having a hot cup of coffee and one of her delicious sweet rolls. The golf cart sloshed out onto the county road and we headed for town.

The ducks sat on the seat beside me, looking out the windshield. I don't know what they hoped to see, but all I saw was mud and soggy leaves. At the Paisley Bridge, I paused to inspect the water level. Wally was right, the river was rising at an

CHAPTER 17

alarming rate. It had overflowed the banks in some spots, and the water was beginning to lap at the roadway. The arches of the cement bridge were normally high enough that a canoe or raft could float under with no problems. Today, there were barely five inches between the abutments and the rushing water. There was plenty of debris, too. Sticks and corn stalks and other detritus swirled and eddied in the muddy river. It was beginning to pile up around the bridge supports. No longer could the larger pieces make it under the bridge.

The noises that the water made weren't the friendly, playful ones I was used to, either. This river was angry. It roared and slurped and acted as if it were a hungry monster of some kind.

Shivering at the image, I bumped across and turned onto Main Street. As I followed the curve around the park, I saw Quinn's work truck over by the pump house/storage shed. I remembered hiding inside of it in the middle of the night, trying to catch a criminal. I spotted some poles in the park that I hadn't noticed before. They had what looked to me like a basketball hoop made of thin chains at the top. I recognized them from the posting I'd seen at the rec center. They must be the disc golf targets.

The usually placid lake in the middle of the park was overflowing its banks, too. Little tufts of grass were poking up through the standing water. I hoped Wally was right about this ending soon. I was going to need a boat to get around town if it didn't.

The bell over the door to Something Nice Café let out a cheerful tinkling sound when I opened the door. I wove between the small bistro tables with mismatched chairs to the glass display case. The walls covered with old advertising pieces and red checkered curtains added to the homey feel of the place. The smell of cinnamon and coffee lifted my spirits. Harvey and Peeper seemed to appreciate it almost as much as I did.

Nora greeted me at the counter as I set down a large crate filled with cream, milk, and eggs. "Thanks for the supplies, Granny. Can I pour you a cup?" Nora was a large woman with an even bigger heart. Her cheeks were round and pink, which caused her eyes to practically disappear when she smiled.

"Yes, please. Do you have time to join me?"

Nora poured two cups and carried them to a table by the window. The ducks trailed after her like puppies. When she sat down, she reached into her apron pocket and pulled out some dried oats and a small dish. They settled under her chair to enjoy their treat.

"Are you going to the Town Hall meeting tonight?" Nora asked. She wrapped her large muscular hands around her mug. Kneading bread dough is apparently a great arm workout.

Sipping the fresh coffee, I said, "Of course! Are you? This foolishness has got to stop."

"Those strangers came in here with their fliers and accosted my customers. I had to kick them out. Who knows if it is true, though. I actually saw a flying object myself Thursday morning. You know how early I have to get here to make the pastries? As I was driving around the lake, I saw something with bright blue lights hovering over the water. I thought at first it was just a trick of the light, you know, like the street lamps' reflection or something. But then it started to move. Lightning struck it out of the sky. I hit the accelerator and got the heck out of there." She shivered.

From the opposite side of the small café came a deep gravelly voice. "I seen one, too."

Nora and I turned to look at who was speaking. Leaning his back against the wall was my neighbor, Earl Foxman. He was holding one of Nora's white mugs in his large calloused hand.

CHAPTER 17

The green ball cap on his head was dirty and greasy, as were the blue coveralls he always wore.

"You saw one? When? Where?" Nora asked.

"Last night. Bright lights movin' 'cross the sky over my farm." He took a noisy slurp from his mug. He had his legs crossed and one arm draped over the back of another chair close by. He squinted his eyes as he looked at us.

I thought about sharing my experience but decided to keep it to myself.

Earl took off his hat and scratched his head. The skin on his forehead was pale, a stark contrast to the deep brown of the rest of his face. Placing the hat back where it belonged, he went on. "I was checkin' on my horses when I seen it. I grabbed my shotgun and fired at it. Winged it good. The thing wobbled a bit and took off 'cross the river toward town." He used his mug to motion out the window. "Looked like it was headin' this way."

"Did you get a good look at it?" I looked from Earl to Nora.

Nora lifted her mug to her lips and shook her head. "I never saw the shape of it, just the lights. I didn't stick around to study it. I don't want to be the unlucky one that gets abducted." She shivered again.

Earl uncrossed and recrossed his long legs. The pant leg on his coveralls rode up, revealing the tops of his scuffed, mud-caked work boots. "Oh, that ain't no UFO, Nora. That's some government spy equipment, I'll guarantee you. They's lookin' over our town for those drug traffickers. The interstate highway bein' just outside o' town, this is a prime spot for one o' them labs. The Feds have heat-seekin' technology to find where they's cookin' that stuff at night. The freaks in town're just amateurs compared to what's really goin' on."

Knowing Earl for as long as I have, I knew it was time to change the subject or get ready for an hour-long lecture on one of his pet topics. High on that list was government corruption. I turned to Nora, "So, I see that you're one of today's giveaway spots. What delicious concoction are you donating?"

"I've invented a SUN butter cupcake that's just divine," Nora replied, clasping her hands together. "I just love the ideas that the Business Alliance comes up with, don't you? Are you going to put your name into the drawing?"

"You know I can't resist your cupcakes," I said. We both stood up and went to the counter. "How about you, Earl? Care to put your name in?"

With a dismissive wave, Earl said, "Nah, I never win nothin'. This here contest is a waste of time. You know they always rig things so they choose who they want to win." He picked up a bear claw from the small plate in front of him and took a big bite. Spraying sugar, he said, "Sun butter sounds made up, anyways."

I shrugged my shoulders and turned to fill out my card. Then sudden inspiration hit me and I reached for another card. Wouldn't Earl be shocked if he actually won?

Chapter 18

The other giveaway box was at the hardware store. I checked my list for what I needed to pick up there. I was on a little bit of a time crunch because I didn't want to leave Spitz at home by himself for too long on his first full day.

I splashed through the gutter and onto the sidewalk with my two waddlers close on my heels. They were really enjoying all the socializing. "Now, remember, we are getting what we need and getting out quickly," I said, more for my sake than theirs.

Some of the uniformed Perigee Prophets were staking out the front door of the hardware store. It seemed that there were more of them every day. This particular group was much more aggressive than the others I'd encountered. They marched around, chanting, and holding up their signs. "Come with us!" I tried to get past them, but one of the greenies stood in my way.

"Do you want to come with us?" she asked. Her eyes darted between my eyes and my chin. Her lime green hair was plastered to her head and her too-large ears stuck out. "The end is near for all who don't listen."

I took her by the shoulders and physically moved her to the side. "No, thanks. I'm not interested." She didn't resist me and actually let me pass. At least she didn't try to give me another paper.

The only thing new about Happy Hardware was the all-glass entry doors. Everything else about the place was from the last century, from the creaky old hardwood floors to the faded advertisements on the walls. Some of the products on the shelves were probably as old as the building itself. In a world of constant change, it was nice to have a few things that stayed the same.

I waved at the young clerk and wandered down the aisles. The ducks were exploring on their own, but I kept an eye on them. Some of the items on the lower shelves might be too big of a temptation for Harvey. He was one of the reasons I was here today. I still couldn't find the brass spray nozzle I used to clean out the watering tanks. I had looked everywhere for it, but it wasn't in any of his usual hiding places. I'm sure I would find it eventually, but in the meantime, I needed a backup nozzle.

I found the replacement quickly and went down another aisle to find light bulbs. There were so many varieties that I had to study the packaging carefully. Did I want 45 watts or 60? Was incandescent better or natural light? Eco-smart? My head was swimming with the options. I just needed to replace a bulb in the bathroom. I was so focused on reading labels that I wasn't watching where I was going. As I backed up to get a better look at the top shelf, I bumped into someone and almost dropped the box I was holding.

Stumbling, I reached behind me for a shelf to hold onto while I caught my balance. My hand landed on the edge of an open box of miniature flashlights, tipping it over and sending all the pieces tumbling to the floor. I managed to right myself before I crashed down among them.

"Oh, excuse me!" I exclaimed. "I'm so sorry." I turned around to pick up the spilled merchandise and clunked heads with whoever I had run into as they also knelt to help clean up. I looked over at my victim. "Why, Wally Teller. We seem to be running into each other a lot this week." I rubbed my head. "Literally."

Wally was dressed the same as he always was, in the oversized blue windbreaker. I could see his clumsy attempt to repair the rip in the sleeve. His dark hair really stood out against his pale forehead in the fluorescent light. The corners of his bright hazel eyes crinkled when he smiled at me. "Do they go everywhere with you?" He pointed at Harvey, who was busily poking his bill into the mess.

"Just about," I laughed. "What brings you out on this dreary day?"

Wally held up a small package in his dirty hand. "Just working on a project. I needed some electronic parts and some LED lights for one of my inventions."

"This doesn't have anything to do with fluffy-tailed birdseed stealers, does it?"

Wally blushed clear back to his receding hairline. "You heard about that, did you?" He fiddled with the item he was holding. "That old lady didn't give me a chance to explain or anything. The police officer made me dismantle it. Said I was lucky he didn't write me a ticket for disturbing the peace."

"I'm sure it worked beautifully," I said gently. I was biting the insides of my cheeks to keep from smiling. He looked genuinely hurt over the incident.

"Oh, yes! The squirrels haven't been back since. This stuff is for a different project, though. I'm working on a way to track rising water." His face became serious. "I'm worried that something might happen in the middle of the night when we can't see the river."

I nodded solemnly. "I agree. I noticed this morning that it has breached its banks. Good luck with that. I hope it works."

As I turned to leave, Wally said, "Hey, Granny? Do you know how many telemarketers it takes to change a light bulb?" He gestured to the box in my hand.

I shook my head.

"Just one, but he has to do it during dinner." His cheesy grin revealed two dimples.

Taking my purchases to the front counter, I looked around for the yellow giveaway box. As the young teenage clerk rang up my items, I filled out my card. A handwritten sign taped to a ruler that stood behind the box said, "Win a hammock today!" Next to the box was another, bigger box with a full-color picture of a happy lady reading a book while lying in a striped hammock. I never had time to lie around, but the thought of being able to take an afternoon off and simply relax made me excited to win.

"Come on, Harvey, Peeper," I called. "Let's get home." My companions made a beeline for the door and waited for me to open it. I pulled my hood over my head and suddenly remembered that I needed to pick up my Dolly Parton wig from the salon for the dance tomorrow night. A lot of good it did me to make lists.

True Colors was just two doors down from the hardware store, so I hustled over, staying under the awnings as much as I could.

As I was leaving the salon, a large black SUV with tinted windows pulled up next to my golf cart. It was shiny and looked brand new. No one I knew drove something that fancy. Most of the big vehicles in town were pickup trucks. It dwarfed my little electric cart and made it look rather dowdy. The driver's door opened and a middle-aged man stepped out, opening an umbrella. He walked briskly over to the demonstrators and singled out one of them. I couldn't hear what was said, but it was clear that the man was giving orders to the group. Well, that was interesting.

The man turned on his expensive heel and headed back my way. Now, I'm not one to meddle in other people's business, but my curiosity was piqued. I stepped in front of him and said, "Howdy!"

He glanced at me and gave a nod. He attempted to skirt around me, but I stepped back in front of him. "Are you new in these parts? I'm Irma Appleton." I stuck out my hand and looked him in the eye.

His shoulders tensed and he flexed his fingers. Suddenly his features relaxed and he smiled. "Glad to meet you, Ms. Appleton. I'm Volans." Again, he attempted to leave, but I held onto his hand.

"That's quite an unusual name, Volans. Are you with those Perigee Prophets over there?"

I inclined my head toward the group that was shuffling down the street, chanting, "Mother take us home!"

Volans' smile widened, reminding me of that green character that steals Christmas. "As a matter of fact, I am their leader. Are you interested in coming with us when the mothership arrives?"

I ignored his question. "How come you don't ... look ... like them? Seems a little odd that you are in such fancy duds and drive an expensive car when they can't even afford a sandwich."

He tugged on his hand and shifted his feet. "I'm late for a meeting." He stormed around me and jumped in his rig.

Chapter 19

Back at the farm, I deposited my shopping bag on the kitchen table and headed out to the barn. I slid the large door to the side and waited for my eyes to adjust to the dim interior. I had put Spitz in the first stall on the left, and I could see him peeking over the half-door at me. His ears were laid back against his head and his eyes were wild and big.

I approached the pen slowly, talking softly to him. He started making a high-pitched sound like a boiling tea kettle, moving his head from side to side. I stopped where I was and waited for him to calm down. He'd exhibited this same behavior this morning. It was going to take some time to earn his trust. That was OK. I had lots of time and nowhere to be. He must have been too far gone last night to remember who I was, or where he was.

Inch by inch, I made my way closer to where Spitz was standing. I used my most soothing voice and thought about getting the portable radio I had used with Pearl. Something else to try. His ears began to perk up a little bit and his breathing slowed. I extended my hand, palm up.

"QUACK!" Harvey announced his arrival in the barn in his usual style, at the top of his lungs with his wings spread out as far as he could get them. Spitz reared back and released a great big gob of green goo. I managed to move out of its trajectory, mostly. He began racing around the stall, kicking at the walls with his front hooves.

I moved away slowly, trying not to alarm Spitz any further. "Thanks a lot, Harvey," I muttered, using my fingers to remove the nasty-smelling stuff from my shoulder. "So much for making progress." The duck nuzzled my hand, happy that I was paying attention to him. He waggled his tail feathers. Sometimes animals can be so sensitive, and other times, so clueless.

Once Spitz quit tearing around his box, I went over to an open hay bale and picked up a flake. By the time I got back to his stall, he was lying down, calmly chewing his cud in that peculiar side-to-side motion that llamas have. He looked at me and then turned his head, almost in a dismissive motion. I guess I know where I stand with him. I refilled the hay rack and checked the level in the water tank. Spitz ignored me completely, which was fine with me. "I named you Mark Spitz after a great Olympic athlete, but you just gave new meaning to the name." I didn't go as far as to shake my finger in his face, but boy, I felt like it. I knew it wasn't his fault, he'd been reacting out of fear. I just wish I hadn't been on the receiving end of his defensive moves.

Chapter 20

"Look what I found today," Quinn said that evening. She plopped something hard onto the kitchen table. I wiped my hands on a dishtowel and walked over to see it.

The object was a white plastic box about 8 inches square with little tiny screws in it. There were wires sticking out of it and it reminded me of a pincushion. I picked it up, surprised at how light it was. I turned it over and noticed that there were sharp edges where part of the object had broken off. I also saw scorch marks.

"Where did you find this?" I asked.

Quinn huffed. "It was blocking one of the grates where the lake drains out into the canal. Looks like a kid's toy. It's bad enough that I have to deal with all the flooding from the rain washing sticks and leaves into the drainage system. I don't need trash thrown into the mix. To top it off, these Prophet people are trying to camp in our park and leave their garbage all over."

I told her about how Nora and Officer Ramos had both seen something flying over the lake get struck by lightning. "I wonder if this is what they saw? By the way, I met the leader of that group today. He wasn't dressed like them. He was wearing a fancy suit and driving an expensive SUV. Something about this whole situation stinks."

CHAPTER 20

"You're telling me. They all have strange names like Neptunia and Celestia. I met a couple of them when they came begging me for some food today. I gave them what I had, which wasn't much. If what you say is true, this sounds more like a money scheme than a true cult."

We ate a quick supper of leftovers while we talked about the strange happenings in town, then got ready to attend the Town Hall meeting, leaving the broken object in the middle of the table like a strange centerpiece. I wanted to go early so that we could get a seat up front. Being barely five feet tall, I hate when I have to sit behind someone who blocks my view.

When we passed the park, I noticed that there were many people milling around. Most of them had bright green hair and flight suits, but there were some regular clothing styles mixed in. Many of them were chanting and carrying their placards, which were starting to droop from getting wet. I could hear, "Today's the day!" It made me sad to think that some of our own people had been sucked into their delusions. Surprisingly, there were no demonstrators at the high school. They were totally focused on their arrival party or whatever they were calling it.

The parking lot was packed. Luckily, my golf cart can fit into small spaces and we parked near the building. The rain was coming down harder than it had before. Quinn and I hurried inside.

Crossing the large open foyer where the school's mascot was painted on the floor, I passed the glass cases filled with sports trophies. I was focused on the open doors to the gymnasium, where there was a steady echo of conversation. We stepped inside and stopped. The place was already filled to capacity. The school had set out chairs on the basketball court and people were milling about, getting settled.

"So much for snagging a good seat," I muttered to Quinn. Even the stands were filling with townsfolk.

She put her hand on my back and nudged me. "Well, let's not just stand here, or we may not even get a chair. I know how much you hate sitting on bleachers."

As we made our way through the crowd, I was scanning for seats. I saw a blue-clad arm waving furiously. Wally's scalp reflected the light from the ceiling. I waved back and tapped Quinn on the shoulder.

"Looks like we'll be able to sit close to the front after all," I said.

We wove through the crush of neighbors and friends. Some of them were smiling and said a friendly word or two. Others looked anxious. A few wore scowls and had crossed arms. This meeting should prove to be a lively one if nothing else. Occasionally, a flash of lightning would brighten the room, then the big overhead lights would dim with a brownish hue before returning to their regular glow. Between the talking and rain beating down on the roof, it was very loud.

It took us a good ten minutes to make it to the row where Wally had reserved seats for us. "I knew you'd be here, Granny, so I saved you a spot," he said proudly. "Hello, Quinn." Wally ducked his head and pushed his glasses up his nose. I noticed his color rise a little, too. But it could have just been the heat and humidity. Sure, it was.

"Granny, do you know why fish are so smart?" Wally was looking somewhere in the vicinity of my shoes. "It's because they live in schools."

I turned to see if Quinn was listening. She rolled her eyes at me and moved to the seat farthest from Wally. I took the seat in the middle and shrugged off my rain jacket.

CHAPTER 20

The noise level had risen to the point where I could see that Wally's lips were moving, but I couldn't hear him. I leaned in close to him and cupped my hand around my ear. "... haven't seen any of these so-called UFOs myself. And I'm outside at night a lot. Have you?"

Nodding my head vigorously, I replied, "Oh, yes! There was one over my farm the other night. It scared my poor donkey half to death. Earl Foxman saw one, too. He even tried to shoot it out of the sky. He thinks he may have hit it with some buckshot."

Wally gave me a strange look and started to say something, but just then, the police chief and the mayor climbed up onto the small platform and sat behind the table that had been placed there.

Mayor Springer had on a short-sleeved oxford shirt in baby blue with tan pants. He looked very nervous, the way he kept tugging on the top button of his shirt, and even from where I sat five rows back, I could see his Adam's apple bobbing up and down.

Chief Ellis looked slightly more relaxed in his blue jeans and a dark gray polo shirt with the badge embroidered on the left side. He was wearing his gun on his right hip and his radio on the left.

The noise in the gym quieted and people shifted in their seats as the last of the stragglers hurried inside.

The mayor pulled the microphone on its short stand closer to his mouth and tapped on it. A high-pitched electronic squeal made everyone groan and cover their ears. Springer raised his eyes to search for the sound booth. He paused for a second, then nodded.

"Sorry about that, folks." He cleared his throat and tugged on his collar. His voice echoed in the large room. "Thanks for coming out tonight. Here's how this is going to work. Chief

Ellis has prepared a few remarks, then we'll open the floor to whoever would like to speak. Use the microphone at the front here." He pointed at the wooden podium that had been placed on the floor in the aisle between the rows of chairs close to where we were sitting. "Each person will have two minutes to either ask a question or share remarks. We've rigged a yellow light to give you a 30-second warning and a flashing red light when your time is up. Donny there, in the sound booth, is instructed to cut off the microphone when the red light goes off to discourage longwindedness." He chuckled nervously and the crowd joined in politely.

"Let's keep this meeting orderly and civilized. Chief Ellis?" He passed the microphone to the chief and sat back. I could see his knee bouncing under the table. For a politician, he sure didn't like big crowds. Or maybe it was the topic at hand. Or what he had experienced the other night.

"Guess that was my cue to keep this brief." He gave a small smile and started reading. He shared the same things that he had told me in his office yesterday. The audience was attentive at first, but the mood shifted when he talked about the new group having constitutional rights to peaceably gather. People started trickling toward the front to line up behind the podium.

"We don't feel that our citizens are in any danger at the moment," the chief said, "but we'd like to get this matter resolved quickly. I have a plan to get more eyes on the sky. I'm here tonight to ask for the public's help. I need volunteers to sign up for different shifts to catch the source of these so-called UFOs." He pointed at several easels that had been set up under the far basketball hoop. Each one held a large piece of poster board. "I'm happy to take any questions, concerns, or complaints that you have."

CHAPTER 20

He set his papers down and folded his hands over the top of them. No shaking limbs or extra swallowing from him. He was as cool as a cucumber.

Wally poked me in the ribs with his elbow. "I like this guy. Calm under pressure. Good head on his shoulders, too. If anyone can catch those things, it'll be him. I'd like to help, but I'm up to my neck in my latest experiment. Are you going to sign up, Granny?"

"Of course, I will," I whispered. "I want those hooligans caught in the act. No one should be allowed to frighten the public like this."

The first speaker at the podium finished what they were saying and the crowd responded by clapping. I'd missed everything they said.

The next several people shared their experiences with the mysterious flashing lights. Some had seen blue ones, some white, some a combination of both. There was a lot of murmuring in the seats around us.

Wally stiffened and grabbed my arm. "What is it, Wally?" I asked, looking at him. His face had gone white and he was trembling. "Are you sick? You don't look well."

"Hide me," he whimpered burying his head in my sleeve.

I glanced around to see what danger had elicited such a reaction. Then I saw who was standing at the podium in all her teased-up hair and polyester pantsuit. It was mean old Mrs. Baker; the woman Wally had scared with his squirrel deterrent air horn. She was holding her precious Pomeranian, Princess Cloe. The dog was wearing a dress with a tutu-style skirt. There were pink bows in the hair over its ears. I thought I caught a glimpse of hot pink nail polish on its claws, too.

"For those of you who don't know me, I'm Beverly Baker,"

came her nasally voice. As if on cue, there was a flash of lightning and the gym lights dimmed again. A roll of thunder rattled the windows set high above the bleachers.

"I've lived here in Paisley Pointe all my life and have never seen such a lazy police force. It's your job to remove the riff-raff. We pay you to protect us and now you want *us* to catch the bad guys? If that's the case, why are we spending our hard-earned tax dollars on you?" She turned to face the crowd. "Am I right?"

There was a smattering of applause, but several "boos" as well. Wally ventured a peek around my shoulder.

The yellow warning light on the table came on. . She pointed a gnarled finger toward the stage. "What do we need you for? If you can't get the job done, then, Mayor Springer, you need to hire someone who can! I don't think –" The red light flashed and the microphone cut off.

Beverly didn't let that stop her. She just kept right on ranting at the top of her lungs. "I have a right to speak. How DARE you! Turn that microphone back on. People, this is a travesty. An assault on my constitutional rights." Beverly's husband, a mouse of a man, was tugging on her beefy arm, trying desperately to get her to sit down. Princess Cloe was yipping loudly.

A murmur went through the crowd and laughter could be heard in several places. The booing increased as Beverly attempted to extricate herself from her husband's grasp. People started moving around and talking to each other.

Mayor Springer reached for the microphone. He raised his voice to be heard over the crowd. "Settle down. Everyone just calm down." He made downward motions with his hands as if that would cause people to follow his instructions. No one was listening to him. The noise level increased and Beverly's shrill

CHAPTER 20

voice could be heard above it all.

More people were surrounding Beverly, trying to calm her down. I saw Tyler Flanders, the fire chief, approach her, putting his hands on her shoulders. Beverly, although shorter than him, outweighed him by at least 50 pounds. She put her free hand out and rammed him right in the chest. Not expecting it, Tyler lost his footing and crashed backward into the folding chairs, his arms flailing like windmills.

Shouts of anger erupted from the people he fell on. More people rushed over to help them. Chief Ellis came down off the stand. Some of the men had gotten hold of Beverly's arms and were attempting to restrain her.

Just as the crowd reached a fever pitch, there was a blinding flash of lightning along with a deafening clap of thunder. Immediately, the power went out, plunging the gym into darkness. Loud cries and screams erupted all over the place. The woman just in front of me screamed, "It's real!" and passed out.

Chapter 21

Chief Ellis's voice echoed over the chaos. "Everyone FREEZE!" he bellowed. The noise level lowered significantly. "Stay right where you are. If you have a cell phone, turn on your flashlight app."

Pinpoints of light began popping up. It looked like stars in a midnight sky. Different ringtones could be heard around the gym. I heard birds chirping next to me and realized it was Wally's phone. "It's my mother," he said to me. He held the phone up to his ear while plugging his other ear with his finger.

I nodded and sat calmly. I didn't understand why everyone was in an uproar. Patience was the key. It was just lights, for heaven's sake. There wasn't a fire or an explosion of any kind.

"Folks, looks like power is out all over town," Chief Ellis's voice boomed out. The sounds of metal chair legs scraping across the wooden floor were loud as people started clearing paths to get to the exits.

Still using his crowd control voice, Ellis said, "Everyone sit tight while we get the emergency generator up and running. You'll be safer in here than out there." The volume on his police radio must have been turned all the way up. Everyone in the room could hear the dispatcher's voice calling him.

"Chief Ellis – Dispatch," the radio squawked. "We have a

CHAPTER 21

missing child. Repeat missing child. Eight-year-old male, blonde hair, blue eyes. Last seen in a backyard on McKinley Street. Child is wearing a red shirt with a cartoon rabbit on it over blue shorts. Name – Alex Rollins."

A collective gasp went through the room. No one made a sound, waiting to see if there was further information. Even Beverly Baker stopped squawking. That was Felix and Betsy's son! An image of the tow-headed child showing me his toy alien spacecraft popped into my head.

"Copy that," Ellis's deep voice was calm and in control. "All available units, drop what you're doing and begin a search with spotlights." As he talked, the chief headed through the crowd back to the platform. He leaped up onto it and turned to face us.

From the back, someone shouted, "How can we help?" Other voices chimed in, asking the same thing.

Now that my eyes had adjusted to the gloom, I could dimly see the chief scanning the crowd. I knew that look. He was formulating a plan. "I'm glad you asked," he said. "You are in no way obligated to help, but if you're willing, here's what we're going to do." Even though most people couldn't see him, he stretched one arm out in front of him. "I'm dividing the gym in half, going down the center aisle. I'm splitting it side-to-side, as well, separating the people on the floor from the people in the bleachers. Quadrants, if you will.

"Tyler Flanders, where are you?" Ellis paused.

"Right here," came the confident voice of the fire chief. He was still up front where he'd been dealing with Beverly Baker, who was back to making a fuss.

"OK, we're going to split the streets of Paisley Pointe into sections, too. Everyone in the bleacher section closest to the main doors, Tyler is your leader. I want all of you to follow him out in an orderly manner and search the area north of Main Street and west of the park. Go now."

It sounded like a herd of elephants as those people called came down from the bleachers and headed out of the gym. The rest of us turned expectantly toward the stage area.

As soon as the first group was out the door, the chief called out, "Officer Baird!"

"Yo!" came the young officer's voice from the opposite side of the room.

"You are in charge of the other half of the bleachers. Take them out and organize search groups for the south of Main and west of the park." Another loud departure. Everyone was calm and moved with purpose. No one was laughing or making small talk.

"Dusty Meadows, I know I saw you in here. Take the group on the floor farthest from the main doors – the group to my right – and head out south and east from Main Street." A quiet departure from this group, but just as determined to help out.

"That leaves you, folks," the chief said, turning toward the area where we were sitting "We will go north and east of Main. Find a buddy to search with. Remember to go slowly and look everywhere."

I turned to Wally, who was fidgeting with the zipper on his windbreaker. "Do you want to ride in the golf cart with us?"

He shook his head. "No, I have an idea..." his voice trailed off as he rushed out the door.

Luckily, my golf cart had headlights. I had them installed when I purchased the cart so I could legally drive it on the streets, along with tail lights and turn signals.

"Where should we start looking," Quinn asked as we climbed inside.

CHAPTER 21

Ahead of us, my headlights reflected off the police stickers on Chief Ellis's rig. "The river," I said through clenched teeth. "I have a bad feeling."

Apparently, Chief Ellis had the same thought. We followed him through town and took Main Street toward home. The whole way we were desperately looking for any glimpse of the child. The heavy rain and lack of street lights made it even more difficult. As we passed the park, I saw that the dirty old camper van had floodlights mounted on the roof. The lights were aimed at the sky and were sweeping back and forth. They also revealed the faces of some of the people closest to the van. I did a double-take as I recognized my friend Divina, dancing to loud thumping music with her face turned up toward the clouds. Shaking my head, I refocused my attention to the more important task at hand.

The police vehicle was equipped with a powerful spotlight, which swept both sides of the street in a pattern. Quinn kept focused on its bright beam as we drove. Every once in a while, she would tense up and point at something, then fall back on the seat when it turned out to be a red trashcan or a bush. We didn't talk but would squeeze each other's hands in silent encouragement.

At the bridge, the chief pulled to the side of the road and stopped. We parked behind him and walked over to the driver's side window. He opened the door and stepped out into the dark, wet night beside us.

"Did you see anything? Hear anything?" I asked. I was hoping against hope that he had pulled over to give us good news.

Shaking his head grimly, Buck said, "Not a thing." He drew his mouth into a tight line.

Quinn and I glanced at each other and then turned toward the sound of the rushing water.

Buck's headlights picked up the dark, moving mass that foamed against the bridge abutments like an angry monster, trying to tear it down. Large tree limbs with the leaves still attached were now tangled together in the water, swirling and bobbing. They looked to me like skeleton hands, clawing at the air. Buck reached inside the police vehicle and brought out two massive black flashlights that looked like they belonged on an aircraft carrier, signaling planes in for a landing.

"Here," he said, handing me one of them. "You and Quinn stay on this bank. I'm going to go over to the other side. If we sweep both sides at the same time, maybe we'll get lucky." He turned to walk across the bridge.

"Wait!" Quinn yelled. She grabbed Buck's arm and pulled him back. She was gesturing into the black sky. "Look over there!"

I followed her arm, thinking she had spotted little Alex. My heart was thumping in my chest and I took a deep breath. I was confused why she was pointing up, though. When I finally spotted what she was looking at, I couldn't believe my eyes. Coming down the river was a UFO. It had red and white flashing lights on the top. Unlike the one I'd seen; this one had a bright light shining down from the underside. It was coming down the river, weaving back and forth, illuminating a patch of light onto the speeding water.

"We don't have time to deal with that right now," Buck said, then stopped. He lifted his flashlight and shone it on the flying object. In the movies, the alien spacecraft are sleek and shiny. They are zippy and can change directions on a dime. This craft was none of those things. It actually reminded me of a bumblebee, the way it wavered and dipped, changing direction as if it had to call ahead and wait ten minutes. Its flight path was anything but graceful.

CHAPTER 21

"I'll be darned," Buck said, putting a hand to his chin. "That thing is sweeping the river."

Sure enough, the crazy little machine was zigzagging from shore to shore, stopping at clumps of willows and shining a light on the debris that accumulated around the roots. It rotated 360 degrees before moving on.

We ran down to the river bank. The UFO was only about 100 yards up from us. Buck's light revealed that it had four propellers on top, spinning fast.

Shouting to be heard over the roaring water, Buck said, "That isn't a UFO, that's someone's rinky-dink drone. Looks homemade to me. Being above the water, it can do a better job of searching than we could. But, the more eyes on the river, the better." He moved off and started across the bridge. Quinn took the flashlight from me and headed for the downriver side of the bridge to search. I searched the shores for whoever was operating the drone, but couldn't see much in the dark.

I turned to follow her as the object came past me. I could tell that it was, indeed a drone. I saw from the light reflecting off the water that a camera had been attached to the underside of it with black electrical tape. It paused and waggled one side up then the other like it was greeting me. The rain was making it very difficult for the little thing to fly straight, but it was getting the job done. It moved off and came to the huge tangle of branches and debris that was crushed against the bridge. The drone began going over every inch of the pile. At one point, it backed up and went over a section again. Then it moved on and continued searching.

I was mesmerized by the thing. It was awkward and clumsy and ugly. It dipped and swayed and turned above the mess. I shook my head at its ingenuity and started after Quinn. Buck was right, time was of the essence and I didn't have time to stand and gawk.

Just as I crossed the road, the drone zoomed past me, right by my head. It stopped, turned, and did its little waggle motion again. I waved at it and kept walking. It came in front of me again, this time spinning around and moving side to side. Then it started back to the upriver side of the bridge. I stopped and stared at it. The drone came back and did its dance a third time. It reminded me of my dog, Wags, when he wanted me to play with him.

A light bulb went off in my head. "You've got to be kidding me!" I muttered to myself. I started back toward the bridge. The drone kept just above and ahead of me, lighting a path to the river. It would pause if I fell too far back. When I arrived at the edge of the water, the drone went out over the tangle of rubbish to a spot that was not quite in the middle, but almost. It paused there and did its dance again.

I squinted and leaned forward. I was wishing I had Buck's powerful flashlight. Not seeing anything due to the distance and angle, I turned and jogged (old ladies like me don't run) up the road to the center of the bridge to a better vantage point. The light on the drone was getting dimmer. Once again, I squinted and then leaned over the railing.

There, in between the leafy foliage, I spotted something. Something red. The drone lowered itself closer to it and I could see movement. Was that an arm? I gasped and reached for my cell phone. I dialed Buck's personal number and stared at the spot. I didn't want to lose sight of it in case the drone left. I wasn't confident that it would last much longer. The light on its belly was getting dimmer and the propellers seemed to be having trouble keeping the drone aloft.

CHAPTER 21

As soon as Buck answered, I started shouting, "Get to the bridge, quick! That drone thing found Alex!"

I could hear huffing and puffing as Buck started running. (He's much younger than me.) "Where do you see him?" he yelled into my ear.

"Upstream side of the bridge, caught up in some tree branches. I'm not sure how we're going to reach him."

I could hear Buck talking on his police radio. I listened as he gave instructions to his officers and requested fire and EMS services to come to the bridge. By the time he'd finished giving orders, he was pounding across the bridge toward me. He reached my side and I pointed out over the railing. He shone his powerful light at the area and pumped his fist in the air. "Yes!" He yelled down to the boy. "We're coming, son. Hang on." I'm not sure if Buck's voice could carry over the rushing water, the rain, and the drone, but if anyone's could, it would be his.

Buck strode off to confer with the rescue team as they began arriving. Soon I could hear the sound of sirens over the rush of the black water.

Flashing blue and red lights reflected off the wet road and the emergency vehicles began arriving. I called Quinn to give her the news. She joined me on the bridge and we watched the rescue operation unfold. I didn't want to leave my spot until I knew Alex was safe. Quinn kept her flashlight beam aimed at the red shirt. Her flashlight was only a little brighter than the drone's spotlight.

The drone stayed in place, too, wobbling more and more, until a shower of sparks flew out of one of the propellers. The other three tried to keep it airborne, but it sank lower and lower toward the river. The operator, whoever it was, must have sensed that their duty was done and they tried to bring the drone to the shore.

It almost made it, too, but the old thing crash-landed among the dead branches right next to the bridge. I made a mental note of where it came to rest and turned my attention back to the firefighters.

I was thoroughly impressed with the speed and efficiency with which our volunteer force operated. They had obviously spent many hours training, but I wasn't sure what equipment they had that could reach the child in his precarious situation. A person with a life jacket wouldn't be strong enough to swim in the current and a boat would be swept away. The shore was too muddy and unstable to walk on. I was thinking they might need to call one of the bigger communities and request a helicopter, but then I saw them back the big ladder truck toward the river bank.

I'd seen the ladder truck when Earl's barn caught on fire and had been amazed at how high it could reach. Now, I was even more intrigued as they extended it horizontally over the swollen river. They couldn't get the heavy truck too close to the bank, it would have sunk into the mud. When the ladder was extended to its fullest length, though, it was almost right over the boy. There were lights attached to the very top of the ladder and they made the area as bright as day. We still couldn't see much from our position on the bridge because of the tangled branches, but I could tell that Alex was half on the tree limbs and half in the water. Occasionally, I could see him squirm and adjust himself.

A very large fireman wearing a yellow life jacket and a close-fitting helmet bearing the name RICK climbed out onto the ladder. Slung over his massive shoulder was a coil of rope and a bright orange adjustable life preserver. He crouched down and bear-walked out over the raging water. Quinn silently reached for my hand and we held onto each other as we watched. I began

CHAPTER 21

praying silently.

The ladder bobbed gently up and down as he moved further from the safety of the truck. Several more firefighters stood by, watching carefully, no doubt ready to move at a moment's notice should anything go wrong. When Rick reached the end of the ladder, I could see his lips moving as he talked to Alex. He sat on the edge of the short railings and uncoiled the rope. He demonstrated how to put the life jacket on and threw it to the boy.

Quinn gripped my hand more tightly as we watched Alex attempt to put it on. He reached out and grasped the flotation tube, pulling it toward him with one hand while holding onto a branch with the other. The orange tube was longer than his arm and the way he tugged on it told me it was either too heavy for him or he was too weak. He managed to get his head through the loop, but every time he tried to put his arm through, he slipped a little and sank down further into the river. I saw him shake his head frantically at the fireman and reach out a hand.

Rick was now kneeling on the end of the ladder. He made motions with his hand to guide the frightened child. The boy tried to follow the directions. I could tell he was doing his best but it wasn't working. It felt like time was standing still. Like we had been out on the bridge watching this rescue for hours. I couldn't imagine what it must feel like being in the cold, dark water.

A hand gripped my shoulder. I turned to see Buck standing next to me. I reached up and covered his strong, calloused hand with my own. His face was drawn and taut, the muscles in his cheeks working like he was grinding his teeth. Buck took his job seriously. I could tell that right then he was thinking that he hadn't done enough, wishing he could do more. I knew because

I was thinking the same thing. It is horrible standing on the sidelines, helpless to do anything but watch.

The boy was making another attempt to get the life preserver around his body. The current was pulling on his lower body, dragging him down. Another firefighter joined Rick on the end of the ladder. He had brought a shorter ladder with him. The two men placed the freestanding one over the end of the truck ladder and lowered the far end down toward the boy. They lashed it in place. Rick quickly put on a harness like the kind people use when they are rock climbing. (Not that I know that from personal experience, but I've seen them.) He attached his harness to the ladder on the truck with metal clips Then, lying on his stomach, he inched his way, head-first, down the improvised ramp.

Buck's hand on my shoulder tightened and Quinn's grip on my hand did, too. We all stood as close to the railing as possible. The rain had slackened to a slow drizzle, making it easier to see what was happening. I'm sure it made it easier on the rescue team as well. I couldn't imagine just how slippery those ladders were when they were wet.

Inch by inch, Rick drew closer to the stranded child. The end of the ladder rested on the pile of sticks, pushing them down under the water as more of Rick's weight rested on them.

"Ooohh, I can't watch this," Quinn said, burying her head in the sleeve of my raincoat.

Soon, Rick's head and arms were just above the mess, right in front of Alex. Hooking his feet between the rungs of the ladder, he grabbed the boy's arm with one hand. With the other hand, he maneuvered the life preserver around Alex's body. I let out the breath that I hadn't realized I was holding. They were making progress but weren't out of danger yet. After snugging the life preserver around the tiny figure, Rick, lying down with his feet higher than his head, put his hands under the boy's arms and lifted him onto the top of the branch pile.

Cheers erupted up and down the bridge and I looked around in amazement. I hadn't realized how many of Paisley Pointe's residents were standing with us, watching. I put my arms around Quinn and Buck and hugged them.

Slowly and steadily, Rick inched back up the ladder with the help of his fellow volunteer pulling on the harness ropes. The child followed him, crawling up the ladder on his hands and knees. I had never seen such a difficult rescue. My stomach was doing flip-flops just thinking about how dangerous it was.

When the excitement was over and the ambulance took Alex away to get checked out at the hospital, Quinn and I said goodbye to Buck, returned to the golf cart, and headed for the farm.

"Wow," Quinn said, "what a night, huh? First, a knock-down, drag-out fight in the town meeting, then a heroic water rescue. Beats watching television, that's for sure!"

I nodded, focusing my attention on the muddy road. "I couldn't agree more. There's just one more thing we need to do tonight before the excitement is over."

"And what would that be?"

"Go fishing!"

Chapter 22

"Fishing? Are you insane?" Quinn's voice was so high-pitched, that it squeaked.

We pulled into the yard and I drove up to the detached garage. Opening the side door, I flipped on the lights. This had been my late husband Chet's favorite space. In here he had tinkered and fixed just about everything you could think of, from kid's bicycles to farm equipment. And if he didn't own a tool, he would make one. I couldn't step inside without picturing him sitting on a stool at the workbench along the back wall with a wrench in his hand, or lying on his back under some vehicle.

His tools and equipment were still here. I had yet to work up the courage to go through his things. Tonight, I wasn't interested in his tools or his workbench. What I wanted was nestled in a piece of PCV pipe mounted on the wall.

Living right on the Paisley River, Chet had whiled away many a lazy summer afternoon, fishing for bluegill and walleye. I never developed a love for the sport, but I would go with him, sit under a tree, and read a book. Those were peaceful times and good memories. His favorite fishing pole was about six feet long and very lightweight. I pulled it out of the holder and checked the line. A large hook that looked like a green one-eyed alien was attached to the end. Perfect.

CHAPTER 22

I turned to go and bumped into Quinn.

"You weren't kidding. You really want to go fishing?"

"Do you still have Buck's big flashlight?" I asked.

She nodded. "It's in the golf cart. I forgot to give it back to him."

"Good. Let's go."

Stowing the rod in the back seat, I punched the accelerator and we slipped and slid toward the bridge. Stopping right at the crown, I set the emergency brake and turned to Quinn. "Grab the flashlight and come with me. We ARE going fishing, but it's not what you think."

We went to the railing and stood almost exactly where we had been watching the excitement earlier. Everyone was gone and it was pitch black. The river was loud and ominous, just feet below us. I traded Quinn the flashlight for the fishing pole and turned it on. The powerful beam showed me that the debris pile had grown and shifted even in the short time we had been gone. Turning toward the town side of the bridge, I traced the shoreline and swept the light across the branches.

There, just where I had seen it land, was what I had come for. The drone. Keeping the light trained on it, I walked along the bridge until we were right above it. I turned to Quinn, who was looking over my shoulder. "Hold the light on it, if you please." I took the fishing pole from her and put her hand on the flashlight, keeping the wrecked equipment in the center of the beam.

"That's some fish!" Quinn exclaimed. "I was sure you were losing it, Granny. But this is genius."

Extending the pole over the railing, I released the strange-looking fish hook and let out some line. I lowered it a little at a time, aiming for one of the propellers. (It sounds easy. Just put the hook under one of the blades and pull it up. That's how they get you to spend all your money on those claw machines at the carnival, too. Just lower, grab, pull. Easy as pie. That must be the worst pie ever.)

Every time I would get the hook close to the drone, the current would shift its raft, or a slight breeze would come up, or, if I was lucky and actually hooked the darn thing, it would slip off the second I put any tension on it.

After an eternity of frustration, with Quinn's help, I actually got a good bite on it. I wanted to haul it up quickly before it slipped off again, but I was afraid that if I went too quickly it might bang into the bridge and fall into the water. So, I settled for somewhere in between, and mentally crossed my fingers. I couldn't actually cross them because it took both hands to operate the fishing pole. The drone was heavier than I thought it would be and took all my concentration to raise it.

As it came up, Quinn reached out her hand, ready to grab onto it the second it was close enough. When it was level with the railing, I walked backward until she could latch onto it.

"I've got it!" she yelled, clutching the hunk of plastic and metal to her chest.

I set the pole down and ran over to her. We gently worked the hook out of the crevice between the propeller and the body of the drone.

Back at the farm, we sat at the kitchen table and stared at our prize. We had put it right next to the broken one that Quinn had found at the park. Looking down on it in the dark rain over the river, I could tell that it had been handmade, but up close and personal, this thing looked about as airworthy as my golf cart. The body of the drone was made of a material that reminded me of the pegboard in Chet's shop, only it was yellow and had tiny holes in it. There were two rectangular pieces that sandwiched

CHAPTER 22

a black box with wires snaking out of it. Two longer, thinner pieces formed an X on the underside and a yellow propeller was mounted on each end. The whole thing was held together with screws and silver duct tape.

One of the propeller arms had black scorch marks and was barely attached. I guessed that was where I had seen the sparks and puff of smoke. Some attempts had been made at waterproofing things, using a moldable plastic of some kind, but it was obvious that water had leaked inside.

"It sure isn't the prettiest drone I've ever seen," Quinn said, leaning close to study it.

I reached out and flipped it over. The underside held a small black camera and a light encased in clear plastic. A red light was flashing weakly on the top of the camera.

Quinn pointed. "I think this thing is still recording!" She waved and smiled.

"Oh, dear," I grimaced, patting at my wet wig. "I never look my best when there's a camera around." I picked up a nearby dishtowel and covered the camera. As I did, two things caught my eye. Something out of place. The entire drone was made up of material covered in tiny holes. Holes that were set at regular intervals, in a pattern. On the underside of the drone, though, there were extra holes. Raggedy holes. Holes that weren't meant to be there. Holes that might have been made by a gun loaded with buckshot.

One of those holes had blasted away most of what looked to be a pair of letters, handwritten on the drone. Possibly a W and a T.

Chapter 23

The rain drummed loudly on the roof as Quinn and I stood in the attic on Saturday morning. The single bulb over our heads did little to brighten the space or Quinn's mood. She was staring at large canvases leaned in neat stacks against the sloping wall. Dust tickled my nose as I watched her struggle with her emotions.

"What are you thinking, Quinn? Do we take them all down to the living room?"

The agent from LuxArt gallery was due to be at the farm soon. When Quinn had left New York, she'd brought the bulk of her work with her. There were just too many of them to display in my small home, so, they had been in storage for months. She had been slowly adding new work to the collection as well. So far, we had sorted the pieces three different times. Once by subject matter, then by medium, and lastly by Quinn's interpretation of quality. In my personal opinion, they were all perfect, but then, I'm biased.

Waving her arms, Quinn said, "No, I just need to make a decision." She bit her lower lip and looked around. "They won't need to see everything. If they want to see more, I can bring them up here, I guess." She picked two canvases and handed them to me. "Let's start with these." She grabbed a few more

CHAPTER 23

and followed me down the stairs.

Quinn paced the floor in the living room while I went to the kitchen to plate some cookies and make some tea. As I stood at the sink filling the tea kettle, a champagne-colored Mercedes coupe with a black soft top slowly made its way into the yard. I watched as a very tan man wearing a black suit picked his way in his leather shoes across the yard. His hair was slicked back into a ponytail. He didn't have an umbrella and dark spots appeared on his expensive clothes.

Wags and Brock barked at him and escorted him to the door. Brock was attempting to sniff the man's pant leg when I reached for the latch to let him in. I couldn't believe my eyes when the art dealer lifted his foot and kicked my dog. Brock let out a small yelp.

"Brock, Wags, come!" I commanded. The dogs slunk past me into the laundry room. I narrowed my eyes at the now-unwelcome visitor. I stood in the doorway and stared at him. "What can I help you with?" I didn't feel one bit bad about the fact that his fancy suit was getting soaked.

"I'm from LuxArt Gallery," he said, holding out a thin, manicured hand.

I stared down at the hand and then back at his face. "Is that so?" I didn't move to let him in.

He cast a look around, took his hand back, and reached into his pocket, pulling out a small card. "Yes, ma'am. I believe Ms. Nicholson is expecting me." There was a hardness around his eyes that he tried to hide with a smile.

I took the card without looking at it and stuck it in my apron pocket. "Are you going to treat my granddaughter the same way you treated my dog?"

"Oh, um, that," he laughed nervously. "I thought it was going to bite me. Sorry about that."

He didn't look sorry to me, but I went ahead and opened the door wider and stepped back. "Come in and wipe your feet. I don't need you tracking mud through my clean house."

He followed me to the living room. "Quinn, the man from the gallery is here." I looked around, but Quinn was nowhere to be found. "Make yourself comfortable. I'll go see where she's scampered off to." I didn't like leaving him there unsupervised, but I went looking for Quinn.

I went down the hall toward the bathroom and heard her thumping down the attic stairs. I reached out to grab the paintings she was carrying. Small hairs had worked their way out of her ponytail and were standing on end around her face. A smudge of dirt ran across the end of her nose. "That agent man is here. I'll take these. You go freshen up."

Returning to the living room I said, "Quinn will be here shortly." Mr. Art Expert was standing in front of one of my favorite paintings. It was a large scene depicting a young girl twirling in a field of flowers. The colors were vibrant and alive. The painting captured a feeling of movement in the petals and I could almost feel the breeze on my face. The child's posture was one of total joy. Agent man's expression let me know that he didn't share my feelings. He had his arms crossed and there was a scowl on his face.

He ignored me and kept on staring at the painting. I set down the canvases I was holding and went to the kitchen to finish with the refreshments. I added a few more cookies to the plate while the water heated. Hopefully, the treats would sweeten his disposition a little, but I doubted it.

"Good morning, sir," I heard Quinn say politely, as she entered the living room. "Thank you for coming all the way

–." She stopped and her tone changed completely. "What are *you* doing here?"

Picking up the serving tray, I hurried to join Quinn. Not that she needed any backup.

"I told you I never wanted to see you again." Quinn had her hands on her hips and she was standing toe to toe with our guest. "You've got some nerve showing your face here, Ricardo."

Ricardo? As in ex-boyfriend art critic from New York? I nearly lost my cookies. Literally. The tray almost slid out of my hands. I quickly set it down on the coffee table.

Ricardo reached out and caressed Quinn's arms. She put her hands on his chest and shoved him backward. "Don't touch me!"

He stumbled a bit but smiled. "There's my feisty girl," he said. "I've missed you." He motioned around the room. "And I've missed seeing your work. Your new paintings are amazing."

"You've missed seeing my work?" Quinn spat back. "You mean the work that you trashed in the press? The work you said was 'childish and uninspired'? Thanks to your write-up in the press, not one gallery would show my work, or even take my calls. LuxArt barely gave me two hours to clear my work out of their gallery. Imagine my surprise when they're the ones that contacted me."

This was all news to me. Quinn had been very guarded about her break-up when she came to stay with me. The atmosphere in the room was decidedly chilly. I attempted to interject. "Mr. Barbieri, I'm Irma Appleton, Quinn's grandmother. Why don't you have a seat."

I might as well have been invisible.

"You had just broken up with me, remember?" Ricardo growled. "I lashed out. So what?" He shrugged his thin shoulders, flipping his limp ponytail behind him.

"So what?! So what? I found out you were dating another woman behind my back. You were just mad that you couldn't have your cake and eat it, too."

"I wasn't *dating* her, Quinn," a wheedling note crept into his voice. "We were just hanging out. You took it out of context. You meant everything to me."

I tried again. Laying a hand on Quinn's arm, I said, "Quinn, let's all sit down, shall we?"

Quinn broke her stare with Ricardo to look at me. After a second, her eyes focused and she shook her head. "Sorry, Granny. I can't deal with this." She turned on her heel and left the room. A minute later, I heard the squeak of the back door.

A nervous laugh bubbled up inside me. "Well, that was awkward." I motioned to the serving tray. "Would you care for a cookie?"

Ricardo's eyes were on the doorway behind me. Without a word, he brushed past me.

The screen door protested again. I stood there, wringing my hands, looking around at Quinn's future. She didn't belong on the farm. She belonged in New York, painting and rubbing elbows with art enthusiasts. As much as I wanted her with me, I knew it would hold her back. With a sharp nod, I followed Mr. Art Agent out into the rain.

He didn't head to his expensive car like I thought he would. He was slip-sliding his way to the open doors of the barn. Good. He didn't give up easily. Neither did I. Maybe we could talk some sense into Quinn.

Ricardo was approaching the hay bale where Quinn was sitting when I got to the barn.

CHAPTER 23

"Can we talk?" he asked softly.

Quinn was breaking pieces of straw into tiny bits. "Why? So you can lie to me some more?"

"I would never lie to you."

"Oh, really? So, all those things you wrote are really how you feel about me? About my work?

The straw shredding was reaching confetti levels.

I slipped around behind Ricardo and busied myself straightening some tools.

Ricardo started pacing, kicking at the straw on the floor. "I was wrong. I was hurt and flew off the handle."

"You ruined me, Ricardo. Words have consequences, you know." I had to strain to hear Quinn's words. I knew that I shouldn't be eavesdropping, but I couldn't help myself.

"I'm trying to fix that, Q. I'm not writing for the press anymore. I'm co-owner of the gallery now."

Quinn stood up. "So, that's your game." She began pacing, arms crossed.

"What do you mean?"

"You want to use me."

Ricardo raised his voice. He flung his arms out. "That's not true. I want to help you." A high-pitched sound started coming from the stall right behind him. I glanced over and saw that Mark Spitz had his ears pinned back.

"Help yourself, more likely," Quinn shot back. "How is it that my painting sold in your gallery without anyone consulting me?"

"It was a test. You know, a gauge of interest. I didn't want to waste your time if it didn't work out."

Quinn turned her back on him. "Oh, how thoughtful of you. Take my work and put it up for sale behind my back. I should thank you." The air was dripping with sarcasm.

"Yes, you should! I can make you rich!" Ricardo shouted. Spitz was getting wild eyes and stomping his feet. The noise emanating from his throat grew louder and more frantic. I started inching my way forward, trying to get between the llama and Ricardo. "You don't belong out here, Q. You belong with me!" He turned around and punched the boards surrounding Spitz's box.

"You really shouldn't do that," I said, but it was too late. Without warning, Spitz let fly a huge glob of sticky green goop. With perfect trajectory, it landed right on Ricardo's face.

Ricardo screamed. A child-like scream, which, of course, allowed some of the foul-smelling stuff to make its way into his mouth. He clawed at his eyes and gagged. I grabbed an empty feed sack and hurried over to him.

The dogs came running, barking their heads off. Peeper and Harvey showed up from one of their mud-puddle explorations, beating their wings and quacking. Quinn was laughing hysterically. I was biting the insides of my cheeks, trying hard to show some empathy. Spitz was racing around his enclosure, kicking at the boards.

"Let me help you," I said, wiping at his forehead.

He grabbed the sack out of my hand. "Don't touch me!" He ran the material over his face, smearing it more than cleaning it. Throwing it to the ground, he stomped out of the barn, scattering animals as he went. He was retching and bending at the waist.

"You'll be sorry about this, Q," Ricardo yelled over his shoulder. He stopped and turned around. "This isn't over." Jabbing a finger in Quinn's direction, he spun back around and misjudged the puddle in front of him. His expensive Italian loafers weren't made to navigate muddy barnyards. Arms pinwheeling, he fell backward, sending a sheet of water flying.

"Aargh!" Garbled noises accompanied his efforts to stand upright. With his ponytail dripping, he wrenched open the car door and threw his ruined suit coat inside.

Quinn and I stood side by side in the doorway to the barn, watching the taillights of the Mercedes bounce their way quickly down the long driveway. I winced when I heard his muffler scrape the ground in one of the deeper ruts. I put my arm around Quinn's waist and drew her in for a hug.

"I don't know what you ever saw in that man to make him your boyfriend," I said.

"He can actually be quite charming," she mused. "When he's getting his way and not covered in llama spit, that is." She turned and walked over to the stall, where Mark Spitz was placidly chewing his cud. She scratched his head, right between his ears. "Good boy, Mark. You saved the day."

Chapter 24

I felt as giddy as a schoolgirl, looking in the mirror. I took my Dolly Parton wig off the stand and pulled it over my gray curls. Smiling at my reflection, I adjusted it and fluffed it until it looked perfect.

There were butterflies in my stomach and I practically danced my way down the hall to the kitchen. Tonight was going to be so much fun!

"You look just like a disco ball, Granny," Quinn said, giving me a hug. "I love the sequined look on you."

I hugged her back and planted a kiss on her cheek. "And you look sleek and stylish. Those boys are going to fall over themselves, wanting to dance with you."

Quinn had chosen a simple, yet elegant little black dress. It hugged her curves and was just the right amount of revealing without being trampy. A black velvet choker set off her slender neck and for once her hair was loose around her shoulders instead of in a ponytail. It hadn't taken much to persuade her to join me in the festivities after the show Ricardo had given us. I think that seeing him put in his place, with his backside in the mud, had done something to help Quinn let go of her past. And I changed my mind – maybe the farm *was* good for her. Maybe there was a way for her to have her cake – or pie – and eat it,

CHAPTER 24

too.

"Ready to go?" she asked, glancing at the rooster clock hanging over the stove.

Reaching for my canvas market bag, I said, "Almost." I gently wrapped the wrecked drones in a towel and lowered them into the bag. "I want to make sure and give these back to their owner tonight."

It felt a little like deja vu, driving back into the high school parking lot. It had only been 24 hours since the town hall meeting, but what a different feeling tonight had. There was excitement in the air and loud music pumping through the open doors to the school. We joined the steady stream of people entering the building. Not a single person had green hair, either.

We walked under an archway made of yellow balloons into the gym. Gone were the folding chairs in rows facing the small stage, which now held a table full of music equipment and two very large speakers on stands. The DJ looked vaguely familiar, but I couldn't place him.

To the right of the doors, a large refreshment table groaned under mountains of cookies, brownies, and other sweets. At the far end of the table was a crystal bowl filled with red punch. Pineapples floated on top.

Divina ran up, squealing. "Don't you two look so beautiful!" She grabbed Quinn and me together and hugged us tightly to her pink satin-covered self. Her hair was piled on top of her head in a mound of curls. "I saved you a spot at our table," she said grabbing our hands and tugging us across the floor.

The mayor was sitting there, looking very pleased with himself. The bright yellow tablecloth was topped with a silver bowl filled with a mixture of red carnations and other blooms. As we approached, he stood and bowed. "Welcome, my ladies. Please join us." He indicated two chairs that had been leaned forward. Quinn and I quickly took off our jackets and made ourselves comfortable.

Sterling went to get us some refreshments. Divina began talking a blue streak about all the preparations that the Business Alliance had made, pointing out the flower arrangements she had made for the event. Quinn got up to talk to some of her co-workers. I grabbed Divina's hands, interrupting her, and said, "What happened last night? I saw you in the park."

Her face turned beet red and her mouth slammed shut. Tears threatened to spill out of her eyes and ruin her perfectly made-up face. She shook her head.

"I'm not judging, just wanted to know what you were thinking." I was still holding her hands in mine and began to gently stroke them with my thumbs.

Divina pulled her hands from mine and reached for a napkin. Dabbing the corners of her eyes, she cleared her throat. "I don't know what came over me. I just got caught up in the moment, I guess. No, that's not right. It was more like covering the bases. I kept thinking, I don't want to miss out if it's real. They were so convincing, you know. I know now that it's not." She looked over my shoulder and sat up straight, putting a bright smile on her face.

Sterling had returned to the table with glasses of punch. The conversation shifted to the Business Alliance and the contest. Divina started jabbering about it.

I scanned the crowded room as she talked. Just about everyone I knew was there, dressed in their finest. The dance floor was full of couples laughing and moving to the beat. I even spotted Quinn in the arms of Dusty's mechanic. I smiled.

Seeing my quarry, I excused myself and left the table. I hugged the wall under the basketball nets, now tilted and raised toward the ceiling out of the way. Smiling and waving, I made my way around the dance floor.

My niece Vivian looked splendid in her green cocktail dress. It brought out the color in her deep brown eyes and lovely coffee-colored locks. She had her hand tucked into the crook of her husband's arm, laughing at something he was saying.

Chief Ellis was a dashing figure in his tuxedo jacket and crisp white shirt. His firm jaw was freshly shaven and his jet-black hair was cut high and tight. Once a Marine, always a Marine. His eyes lit up when he saw me approaching. It struck me that they were the exact same shade of green as Vivian's dress.

"Granny, you look amazing," he said, leaning down to hug me.

"Not as amazing as your wife. Keep a close eye on her tonight, Buck or one of these other fellas might try to persuade her to go home with them."

Buck laughed and placed a protective arm around Vivian. "They'd have a fight on their hands if they tried."

The music was loud and thumping through my shoes. It was hard to hear without leaning in close enough to smell the other person's breath. I pulled Vivian down to my height. "Mind if I borrow Buck for a minute? I need to give him something."

She smiled and shook her head. "I'll go grab us something to drink. It's getting a little warm in here."

Motioning to Buck, I walked over to the steps leading up to the small platform where the DJ was bobbing his head to the beat of the music. Who *was* he? It was driving me crazy that I couldn't remember where I'd seen him before.

Once we were behind the speakers, it was a little bit easier to hear. I took my market bag off my shoulder, set it down, and zipped it open. Without removing the contents, I peeled back the towel and showed Buck the drones.

Chapter 25

The evening was everything I had hoped it would be, and more. I had no shortage of dance partners and was cheek-to-cheek with Dusty Meadows when the music stopped. Mayor Springer took the microphone.

Sterling was smiling from ear to ear and took a hankie from his back pocket to mop the sweat from his forehead. His tie was loose and the top two buttons of his striped shirt were undone. I don't think I'd ever seen him that relaxed.

"Is everyone having a good time?" he asked, cupping his ear. Loud clapping and whistling filled the gym. He scanned the crowd, nodding and pointing at a few people. "Let's hear it for our DJ, Officer Javier Ramos! Who knew that our police force was so multi-talented?"

The crowd gave an enthusiastic round of applause, along with hoots and hollers. Javier pumped his fist in the air and grinned. His oversized basketball jersey and backward baseball cap made him look less like an officer of the law, and more like a delinquent teenager. No wonder I hadn't recognized him!

"Before I turn the mic over to Hershel Roman to announce the winner of the big weekend giveaway, I want to acknowledge all the businesses who donated prizes to make this such a fun week." Another deafening round of applause made its way through the crowd. "It makes me proud to be a part of this community," he said, his voice growing husky, "to see such support and camaraderie among our citizens." He touched a hand to his heart and bowed his head.

Behind the mayor, the bank president clapped his hands and nodded. Hershel was shorter than Sterling and . . . how should I say this . . . more girthy. When he smiled, his round cheeks made his eyes disappear. Like they were doing now.

He took a step forward to take the mic from Sterling but paused when Chief Ellis bounded up the steps and caught his elbow. Buck whispered in his ear. A surprised look crossed Herschel's face and he nodded quickly, motioning for the chief to take the mic.

"Wonder what that was all about," Dusty muttered, leaning down to speak into my ear.

Spotting my bag in Buck's hands, I smiled and said, "We're about to find out." I clasped my hands under my chin.

Buck set the bag at his feet and scanned the crowd. In his booming voice, he said, "Good evening, folks. I know you are all anxious to find out who won the grand prize, but I hope you'll indulge me for a second. Is Wally Teller here? I thought I spotted him earlier."

We all turned to look around. "He's right here!" someone near the doors yelled.

"Wally! Would you come up here, please?" Buck called.

The crowd parted and made room for Wally. I almost didn't recognize him in his dress shirt and slacks. I was so used to seeing him in his battered old windbreaker and sweatpants. He looked like a kid dressing up in his dad's clothes. His bald spot was shiny with sweat and his face was beet red by the time he climbed the platform steps and stood next to the chief. He stuck

CHAPTER 25

his hands in his pockets and stared at his shoes.

Buck put his arm around Wally's shoulders and turned to the crowd. "Folks, Hollywood has made innumerable movies about superheroes. I'm here to tell you that they all got it wrong. Superheroes don't wear capes and masks. They wear blue jackets with white letters on them. Here in Paisley Pointe, we have a genuine hero by the name of Wally Teller. You all know him for his weather forecasts on WPLY. And for his jokes and his . . ." Buck coughed, ". . . creative inventions."

A ripple of laughter filled the gym. Buck leaned down and took one of the drones out of the canvas bag. "What you might not know, is that this invention," he held the machine over his head, turning it this way and that, "saved the life of a child last night. Young Alex Rollins was swept down the river and Wally found him. The boy's at home resting now, and is doing just fine."

Several people in the crowd gasped. Dusty said, "Well, I'll be a monkey's uncle." I simply beamed up at Wally.

"It has come to my attention that Wally was working on a device to monitor the rising water in the Paisley River. All those UFO sightings around town were just Wally's drones. Our visitors from out of town had nothing to do with it. He quickly adapted one of them for the search last night and was able to use it to spot Felix and Betsy's son, alerting us to his position."

The crowd exploded in applause. I didn't think that Wally could turn any redder. In fact, he looked slightly purple under all the attention. Buck handed the homemade drone to him and Wally hugged it to his chest. When the crowd settled down, Buck continued. "Wally, on behalf of the Rollins family and the entire community of Paisley Pointe, we thank you."

In the midst of the clapping, Wally turned, scuttled off the stage, and headed for the exit. He didn't make much headway due to the number of people who wanted to either shake his hand, pat him on the back, or hug him. If I wasn't so proud of him, I probably would have felt sorry for his embarrassment.

A cough in the mic brought my attention back to the stage. Herschel Roman, the bank president, said, "Well, that's going to be a tough act to follow, isn't it?" He laughed. "Nevertheless, it is my job to pick the winner of the all-inclusive, three-day weekend trip to sunny Florida." He motioned to two young men standing off to the side of the stage. They were carrying a large box between them that was covered with yellow paper. Judging from the muscles straining the fabric of their shirts, it was brimming with entries. They set it down with a thunk and hustled off the stage.

"I'll just stir this up a bit," Herschel said, bending over the box. He was holding the mic so close to his face that everyone could hear him breathing as he rustled the papers.

It was quiet in the gym as we watched. From somewhere behind me, I heard someone start chanting. I couldn't quite make out what they were saying, but several more people picked up the chant and it grew louder. They were saying, "Wally! Wally! Wally!"

More people started chanting and at the same time, they stomped their feet. Herschel glanced up from the box where his right arm was buried. He was frowning. Taking his arm out and putting the mic on a stand, he walked over to the mayor and the police chief. The chants grew louder and louder. I added my voice, "Wally! Wally! Wally!"

The three men on the stage turned their backs and appeared to be holding a conference. Sterling waved his hands. Herschel and Buck were shaking their heads. After a few minutes, they straightened up. Herschel turned back to the crowd and held up his hand. The gold ring on his pinky winked under the lights. It took several minutes for him to gain everyone's attention.

When the audience was sufficiently quiet, he held the mic up and said, "It seems that there is a motion on the floor to give the grand prize to Wally Teller. Is there a second to the motion?" At least a dozen voices yelled back, "I second!"

"All in favor of granting the weekend getaway to Mr. Wally Teller, say aye."

As one voice, the citizens of Paisley Pointe shouted, "Aye!" I felt my eyes prick with tears.

"Anyone opposed to this, say nay." You could have heard a pin drop. Not even a rustle of fabric.

"Motion carries," the bank president said, his voice husky with emotion.

In the midst of thunderous applause, Wally was pushed toward the stage once again and practically lifted up the stairs by those nearest him. He was still holding the battered drone. The mayor shook his hand, then the chief, and finally Herschel. Taking an envelope from the inside pocket of his jacket, he turned to Wally. "Son, you've earned this prize and deserve it more than anyone here. With compliments of the bank and the Paisley Pointe Business Alliance, enjoy!"

As Quinn and I stepped outside to make our way home, we stopped to look up at the sky. A full moon and some bright stars were shining down from a ragged break in the cloud cover, making everything around us sparkle like diamonds.

A shooting star appeared, but I knew that all my wishes had already come true. There were no UFOs plaguing Paisley Pointe, the rain had ended, and Quinn had put her awful past behind her. Now if I could only find where Harvey had hidden that blasted spray nozzle!

Mini Peanut Butter Pies

Makes about 30 mini pies
Adapted from InspiredbyCharm.com

Ingredients For Chocolate Crust:
- 2 cups all-purpose flour
- 4 tablespoons unsweetened cocoa powder
- 4 tablespoons sugar
- 1 teaspoon salt
- 1 stick unsalted butter (cold)
- 4 tablespoons shortening
- 2 large egg yolks
- 6-8 tablespoons ice water

Ingredients for Filling:
- 1 cup creamy peanut butter
- 8 ounces cream cheese (softened)
- 1 teaspoon vanilla
- 1 ¼ cup confectioner's sugar
- 8 ounces whipped topping (thawed)

Ingredients for Chocolate Drizzle:
- 1 cup semi-sweet chocolate chips

1 tablespoon shortening
Chopped peanuts (optional)

Directions:

1. Combine flour, cocoa, sugar, and salt either with a pastry fork or in a food processor until blended. Add the butter and shortening until the mixture resembles coarse crumbles. Add the egg yolks and ice water and mix until dough forms a ball. Start with about 5 tablespoons of water and add more until the mixture comes together.
2. Press the dough into 2 flattened discs. Wrap in plastic and refrigerate at least 40 minutes.
3. Preheat oven to 350 degrees F.
4. On a floured surface, roll out your dough to about 1/8 inch thick. Then cut out the dough using a circular cookie cutter. (You could get fancy and use a flower-shaped one). Make sure it is about 3 inches in diameter. Once the first set is cut, ball up the remaining dough and roll it out again. Repeat until you have used as much of the dough as you can.
5. Gently press the shaped dough into an ungreased mini muffin pan. Go slow as they may tear. Bake at 350 degrees F for 12-15 minutes.
6. Allow the mini shells to cool completely before removing them from the pan. That way they will maintain their shape.
7. While they are cooling, mix up the peanut butter pie filling. Beat the peanut butter with the cream cheese and vanilla until smooth. Then add the confectioner's sugar, beating again until smooth. Add in the whipped topping and beat the mixture one last time until smooth.

8. Place the mixture in a piping bag or large plastic bag (snip off a small piece of one corner – works great). Pipe into the cooled shells.
9. Make the drizzle by melting the chocolate chips and shortening in the microwave or in a double-boiler. Allow the mixture to cool slightly, then transfer to a piping bag or plastic bag. Drizzle onto the filled pie shells. (Tip: put a piece of waxed paper under the pie shells before drizzling to make clean-up easier) Top with chopped peanuts as a garnish if you wish.

I like to put them in the refrigerator for 30 minutes to firm up the filling before eating.

More Pie?

Granny Appleton would love to make you some more pie. Would you do something for her (and me) in return? Writing a review of the book you just read only takes 5 minutes, much less time than baking something delicious!

It would help her gain the attention she deserves and the incentive she needs to continue baking.

Honest reviews are like slices of pie to this author. I would be so grateful to you if you would leave a few words on my book's Amazon page.

Thank you so much! I can't wait to share Granny's next adventure with you.

About the Author

Missy Tarantino is a full-time teacher in Northern Colorado. She works with children who are just learning English and come from all over the world.

When she isn't in the classroom, you'll find her out having adventures of her own. She is an amateur race car driver and loves going fast on autocross courses.

You can connect with me on:
- https://www.missytarantino.com
- https://www.facebook.com/missywritesbooks

Subscribe to my newsletter:
- https://landing.mailerlite.com/webforms/landing/n4c0t4

Also by Missy Tarantino

Granny Appleton loves her community. She keeps a close eye on what goes on there. Don't try to pull the wool over her eyes. She's already been there, done that, and baked a pie for it!

Duck Down
Making the bullseye isn't the problem. Figuring out who did it is.

Paisley Pointe is a quiet farming community. Nothing much happens there. When the new director for Paisley Pointe's recreation center announces an archery competition, Granny is all for it. But not everyone in town shares her enthusiasm, especially Early Foxman, who is very vocal about his opinions on change.

When Earl's barn catches fire in the middle of the night, tensions flare. Was it an accident or was it arson? With the help of her two companions, Harvey and Peeper, both rescue ducks, Granny puts on her spy hat, and favorite wig, to figure it out.

Can she solve the mystery without becoming a suspect herself or becoming the next victim?

If you like clean, wholesome cozy mysteries with a side of pie, then you'll enjoy this first book in the Granny Appleton series.

Robber Ducky

A Founder's Day celebration gone wrong. A klepto duck with an eye for shiny objects. Does Granny have what it takes to bring down the thief?

Granny is focused on training for her first 5k race. Telling her she can't do something is a guarantee she's going to succeed. When she is bowled over during the race by a jewelry thief, Granny will do everything she can to run him down.

Getting the brush-off from law enforcement pushes Granny to step in and get nosy. She comes up with a plan to get up close and personal with the investigation. But with so many suspects, will she be able to weed out the thief?

Robber Ducky is the third duckumentary in the Granny Appleton Cozy Mystery series. If you like reading about quirky, wig-wearing grannies and rescue animals with cute personalities, then this is the book for you.

<u>**Buy Robber Ducky today and give the jewel thief their own pair of bracelets.**</u>

Quacking the Case
A felon on the loose. Fear in the community. Will Granny fall victim or save the day?

It's harvest time on Granny's farm and she's up to her elbows in apples. When the chief of police tells Granny there's a convict in the area, she shrugs it off. But when Granny realizes she isn't alone in the orchard, she sees things differently.

Granny keeps her head on a swivel and a shotgun nearby. A light in the orchard at night confirms her suspicions. Will Granny catch the felon before he takes her out?

Quacking the Case is the fourth book in the Granny Appleton series. If you like cozy mysteries, then you'll love this one.

www.ingramcontent.com/pod-product-compliance
Lightning Source LLC
LaVergne TN
LVHW010300260326
834688LV00044B/1378